# FIRECRACKER

## DAVID ISERSON

razOr
bill

An Imprint of Penguin Group (USA) Inc.

razOr
bill

Published by the Penguin Group
Penguin Group (USA) Inc., 375 Hudson Street, New York, New York 10014, USA
Penguin Group (Canada), 90 Eglinton Avenue East, Suite 700, Toronto,
Ontario M4P 2Y3, Canada (a division of Pearson Penguin Canada Inc.)
Penguin Books Ltd, 80 Strand, London WC2R 0RL, England
Penguin Ireland, 25 St Stephen's Green, Dublin 2, Ireland (a division of
Penguin Books Ltd)
Penguin Group (Australia), 707 Collins St., Melbourne, Victoria 3008, Australia
(a division of Pearson Australia Group Pty Ltd)
Penguin Books India Pvt Ltd, 11 Community Centre, Panchsheel Park,
New Delhi–110.017, India
Penguin Group (NZ), 67 Apollo Drive, Rosedale, Auckland 0632,
New Zealand (a division of Pearson New Zealand Ltd)
Penguin Books, Rosebank Office Park, 181 Jan Smuts Avenue,
Parktown North 2193, South Africa
Penguin China, B7 Jaiming Center, 27 East Third Ring Road North,
Chaoyang District, Beijing 100020, China

Penguin Books Ltd, Registered Offices: 80 Strand, London WC2R 0RL, England

ISBN: 978-1-59514-370-9

Published simultaneously in Canada

Library of Congress Cataloging-in-Publication Data is available

Printed in the United States of America

10 9 8 7 6 5 4 3 2 1

For Allis.

# CHAPTER 1

# THE KRIEGER ESTATE

**M**y grandfather liked to say, "The only time you are ever truly alone is when you are dead." And I thought that was perhaps something to look forward to as I sat among my bags and trunks on the steps outside the front door of the Krieger Estate. That's what my family's house is called: "the Krieger Estate." My grandfather called it that because he wanted to come up with a really good name, something big and meaningful, but he never did and so he ended up picking nothing.

I really don't know how long I was sitting outside. I figured someone would come out to look for me at some point—they should've been informed by the school that I was coming home. But it was hours before anyone emerged. It had just begun to get dark when my mother opened the front door.

My mother's name is Viviana Mary Elizabeth July Krieger but people call her "Vivi," even me and my sister,

Lisbet. I don't know what it would be like to call her "Mom," and it would be even stranger to call her "Mommy," like some weirdos still call their mothers. She has never come out and said that she doesn't want people to think she's a mother (because that's probably not the case), but she certainly doesn't want people to start mathematically determining her age if they ever realize that she has given birth to a now seventeen-year-old (me) and a now twenty-year-old (Lisbet). Vivi spends four weeks every year going "skiing," and she returns at least four years younger. If she is not getting plastic surgery, she is surely a vampire.

Vivi didn't come out the door for the purpose of greeting me. She came out to smoke. She didn't smoke anything fancy or imported. She smoked off-brand menthol cigarettes. They smelled like Tic-Tacs, and her smoking was a secret. So when she saw me, she hugged herself with her arms as if to say that she had come out for a little fresh air and nothing else. She didn't really look at me. She just nodded at nothing and stared across the driveway. "You're home from school already, Astrid?"

"I'm done. I've learned everything," I said.

Vivi frowned. She'd never really found me all that funny. "There's no point in making up a story. They called us. At least Lisbet will be happy to see you."

"Eh," I said. "Lisbet is happy about everything."

This is true. This wasn't just me being a jerk. Almost everything made Lisbet happy. When I was four and Lisbet was six or seven, our nanny would spend way too many hours at the bus station because Lisbet loved looking at buses. I guess kids are fascinated by all sorts of things, but the buses weren't even moving. They were just parked. "Look at all those wheels," she would say. It was this wide-eyed joy about every single thing that had led her to get engaged so young. I have no idea why else she would be in such a rush to get married. A lot of people get married at twenty, but usually not rich people.

The house felt cold the second I walked through the doorway. It always did. This was the consequence of houses too large for the amount of people who live there. There would have to be fifty people living in the house for it to feel perfect.

"Sam," Vivi said into an intercom next to the front door. "There are bags on the steps that need to be taken in." She turned to me. "We have a new Sam. He's from Sierra Leone." She was talking about a butler. Apparently there used to be another butler named Sam, and she wanted to make sure I knew there was a difference, I guess in case I started a conversation with Sam about the old times. I didn't remember another butler named Sam, though. I never spent a lot of time living in the house, and certainly not long enough to know the name of everyone who ever worked there. I remembered Eda, who was one of my nannies. She was from Turkey and had long black hair and would feed me candy even though Vivi didn't allow candy in the house. I have no idea what happened to Eda.

"We are about to start dinner," Vivi yelled over her shoulder. "So sit down if you want." That was how I was welcomed back home.

>>>>>>>>>>>>

The Kriegers first came to America in the seventeenth century to seek a new life. Back in Germany a couple members of the royal family had been poisoned, and the Kriegers probably did it, so it was a good idea for the family to vamoose from the old country.

America was the land of opportunity, and my ancestors seized it. As some of the earliest settlers, we were part of the very first group of influential and successful people. Back then, we were rich, but soon enough, we were *really* rich.

First we owned plantations.

Then gold mines.

Then railroads.

Then airlines.

Somewhere in there, the family lost all their money and my grandfather grew up poorer than the last ten generations. But he restarted the company to build weapons. Big, destructive, blow-every-single-thing-up weapons. And then the Kriegers became really, *really* rich. And blah, blah, blah, lots of things happened in between. It's called history. Go to the library and read a book about it. People lived and they died. For the purposes of this story (because it's a story about me, Astrid Krieger), all you really need to know about my family is that we have always been what people would like to call "the bad guys." If you ever hear anyone talk about how "The Man" is responsible for all sorts of evil that happened in this country and the world—well, they're pretty much describing the Kriegers.

There's a portrait of my whole extended family that hangs over the main fireplace from about four years ago. It's a huddled mass of grey and blond people with red ties and tight, fake smiles. My little brother, Fritz, is even in the picture, even though he had died several years before the portrait was commissioned. It's the only proof in the entire house that he even existed. The only real evidence that anything might be wrong with the family is me. In the portrait I am lurking off to the side—one of the few Kriegers with dark hair—and wearing my favorite expression: a half smirk with eyes rolled high. I have no idea why

I ended up that way in the portrait. Yes, that's the way I looked that day, but it's a painting. The painter could've done anything he wanted with me. I actually love that portrait because even caught on canvas, I look like I don't belong with those people, and everyone who sees it can tell that I didn't want to be there.

At the center of the painting is my grandfather, Montgomery Krieger, looking serious and clutching an American flag. He is the second-oldest US senator ever. He has pretty much had his hands in everything bad that happened anywhere since World War II. As a result, he learned how to avoid getting caught doing bad things. When I was six years old, he taught me what an alibi was and to always have one handy. "Tell them you were with me," he would say. "And if I have any problems, I'll tell them I was with you." This has helped out plenty for both of us in years since.

Grandpa was old and had a woman working for him full time who was responsible for his feeding and hygiene. Sometimes he referred to her as his nurse. Other times, he called her his "girlfriend." Either way, he would often elbow whoever was sitting next to him and say, "Isn't she buxom? Like a winding road." At the dinner table the night I returned, I happened to be the person sitting next to him.

"Yeah, she really puts it all out there, doesn't she?" I said.

He looked up from his soup at me and asked no one in particular, "Has she been home all this time?"

"It didn't work out in the end with Astrid and the Bristol Academy," my father said. He had a way of putting a simple and bright spin on a situation that wasn't simple or bright.

"They didn't share my imagination as far as what a proper education should entail," I said.

"They caught her cheating. She stole tests and term papers," Vivi said. "And didn't you try to burn down a classroom?"

"That's false," I said. "Well, more or less. It was just time for me to go. It's actually a good thing because I really need some time off. You know, to spend a little time with me."

"But that's great too," Lisbet said. "You can help with wedding planning. You remember Randy, right?" she asked as she reached her hand over to Randy, apparently her soon-to-be husband. I didn't remember Randy. I still don't.

"Oh, if I can fit it in. Depends where I go next." I turned to my father. "Can I go to a school in Switzerland again so I can get my needs more properly addressed?"

That was the scenario that I was most excited about as I'd considered my options while being driven home from Bristol. I felt like I needed an ocean and a few thousand miles of distance from my life of the past few years.

Dad made a noise but nothing really came out, and I could feel Vivi staring at him. Unlike all the other Kriegers, my father, Dirk, was never a bad person. He's the CEO of Krieger Industries, and probably the worst thing you could say about him is that he isn't actually very smart. He wanted to be CEO of the company so he could play with toy airplanes and rocket ships all day. And that's pretty much what he does.

"You're going to live at home," Vivi said.

"That doesn't make sense," I said. "How will I be able to live at home and get to my classes all the way in Switzerland?"

"I don't think you understand, Astrid," Dad said.

"I don't think *you* understand how far away Switzerland is, Dad."

"What I mean is that you're going to go to school here."

"I think she knows what you mean, Dirk," Vivi said. "She's joking."

Dad nodded, reminding us all that he doesn't really get jokes unless they involve farting. "We've decided that we're not going to drop money into your education if you are not going to take it seriously," Dad said.

"Fair enough," I said. "It's time I began living a life of leisure anyway. None of us are getting any younger." I then stared for a little too long at Lisbet. She didn't notice.

"No, we're going to give you structure." Dad wrapped his lips around the word like it was a new toy. "You are going to live here, and you're going to school."

"Come on. Lisbet doesn't do anything and she lives here."

"I have a job," Lisbet said. "I'm an actress *and* a yoga instructor."

"Those are barely jobs," I said.

"Lisbet is also getting married," Vivi said.

"So I need to get married or get a job?" I said.

"You are too young to get married," Dad said.

"But you're also not a little girl. You need to be in school or work." Vivi had this thing about working and the necessity of doing it even if you don't need the money. She would always say things about how I don't have any values because she worked herself through school and all that bootstrap-pulling crap, but she hadn't worked since before Lisbet was born. True, I'd never had a job, but she hadn't had a job for way longer.

"But how can I be in school if you're not going to pay for me to be in school? You're contradicting yourself."

"We think you should go to the public school," Dad said.

This was just a horrible, mean thing to say. Just hearing the words "public school" out loud made my mouth taste like urine (which, not coincidentally, is exactly how the public school smells). "Are you kidding?" I asked.

"No," Dad said.

"I went to public school," Vivi said. "I think it taught me values that you just can't learn by having us spend money on you." She then adjusted the cuff of her blouse, which probably cost four thousand dollars.

"The problem is in the name. I mean, 'public school.' It's full of the public. I'm not a fan of the public."

"It's that or nothing. Think of it as a great adventure," Dad said.

We had reached an impasse. My parents did have some control over where I lived and where I went to school. I'm sure I could have found a way to wrest back that control, but then I wouldn't get money from them, and I would have to get a job anyway.

"Fine," I said. "But if I go to public school, then I don't have to live in the house. I can live in the guesthouse."

"Randy and I live in the guesthouse," Lisbet said.

Because of course they did. How could they possibly live anywhere else on her lucrative actress/yoga instructor salary? I could've sworn Randy had a job. What was it? Something with leaves? Did he study leaves? Was that a job?

"Fine," I said. "Then I get to live in the rocket ship." Five years ago, Dad brought home a prototype of a Krieger Industries rocket ship; rather, a giant truck brought it home. It was full-sized and had all of the buttons and compartments a real rocket ship would have if it were going to space. I suppose it really could go into space with the proper launchpad, fuel, and wiring. Vivi hated everything about it and had the landscapers build a wall of bushes around it so you couldn't even tell it was there unless you got really close. But that actually made it better—it wasn't just a rocket ship; it was a secret rocket ship. Dad set up a television and a refrigerator in the cockpit and he could stay in there for hours if he wanted, maybe even days.

"Not my rocket ship," Dad said, actually whining like a child.

"Who cares? It doesn't even work," Vivi said.

Dad took a deep breath. "Fine. It's a deal. You can live in the rocket ship. But you also have to see a psychologist."

"You think I'm crazy?" I said.

"No. A lot of not-crazy people go to therapy," Vivi said.

Then Dad just stared for a moment as he tried to think of a not-crazy person who was in therapy. "We already found someone to see you," he told me. I had a sinking feeling in my stomach. I'd only been expelled from Bristol six hours before. It didn't seem likely that they'd spoken to a wide array of psychologists during that time. I had a feeling they'd only spoken to one person all day about me, and I didn't like what that meant.

"Dean Rein?" I asked.

My father looked at Vivi. He was terrible with names. "He's the therapist at Bristol, right?"

"He's not a *real* therapist. He just says that to make himself feel smart or something," I said. "We hate each other. Hate. He's my actual, honest-to-god archenemy."

"I think you're being a little dramatic," Vivi said.

"No I'm not. He's the one who had me kicked out of Bristol."

"No," my grandfather said. His attention once again drifted away from his soup. He motioned for the nurse to bring him a cigar and a lighter, which is something I imagine no nurses are actually supposed to do, but she nonetheless had both of those things in her pocket and seemed happy to oblige. I don't know how long he'd been listening to the conversation, but he stared at me, then examined his pinky finger, and then turned back to me. Everyone at the table looked at him nervously. "*You're* the one who had you kicked out of school," he finally said. "Things are about to change, huh, Chickadee?" And he was right. Things were about to change. If nothing changed, I wouldn't be writing this down because this is a book about the time when everything changed. And isn't that what every book is about? No, seriously, isn't it? I don't know. I don't read books.

# CHAPTER 2

# FIRECRACKER

I pushed my grandfather in his wheelchair along the stone walkway that led out to the main pool. The pool was shaped like a kidney with a deep, black pit in its center, modeled after my grandfather's own kidney after he got shot during World War II.

"So, let me get perspective," he said. "Did you cheat?"

"Of course I did. Everyone does."

"Be glad I'm not working for the FBI. The confessions roll right off your tongue," he said. "Were you sloppy?"

"I'm never sloppy."

"Most people get caught because they're sloppy."

"Good for them. I'm not most people. I have no patience for those who can't execute a plan with elegance," I said.

"Indeed. Survival isn't a race. It's a dance."

"I was set up."

"That only means you went into business with the wrong people. You made your bed, Astrid."

"Untrue. I've never made my bed in my life."

My grandfather laughed. I was one of the very few people who could make him laugh.

I knew that if my grandfather told Dad that going to the public school and therapy was a stupid idea, my dad would probably also think it was a stupid idea. But Grandpa was never going to tell Dad that. We both knew it, and I would never ask. He just said, "You got caught. You have to pay if you get caught." He then proceeded to cough for two full minutes.

"Would you do it? I mean, if you were me, would you even listen to them? You would never go to the crappy school, right?"

"I," Grandpa said as he rolled his now-unlit cigar around his mouth, "would never get caught. So it's not really an issue for me, baby, now is it?"

"I guess not."

The Bristol Academy was in Southboro, Connecticut, about an hour away from where my family lived. There were parts of the school I never spent any time in—the tennis courts, the entire third and fourth floors of the library, the kayak dock—but I spent a lot of time in Dean

Rein's office. My first day at Bristol was also Dean Rein's first day as Dean of Students. I had spent the previous day in jail for trying to sell the Southboro Police Station to the People's Republic of China (long story). It was a joke, but some people don't get jokes. I was released quickly, though, because I was fifteen and it's hard to keep a fifteen-year-old in jail for very long. Dean Rein called me into his office as soon as I dropped off my stuff in my dorm room.

"Boy," he said, "wasn't I surprised when I heard one of our new students was in jail."

"Were you?" I asked. "I wasn't surprised. I've been to jail before. The cell had a TV. It was a pretty doable afternoon."

"I was curious about you and so I spoke with Madame Brichot, your last headmistress."

"Oh yeah, Judy, right? How's her leg?"

"Why?" He suddenly got nervous. "Did you do something to her leg?"

"No. Course not. She just had a weird leg."

"Have you not been happy in your previous schools, Ms. Krieger?"

"I don't know. I'm good."

"Your test scores, your grades—they're impressive— but then I look at all of these disciplinary problems and

I say to myself, 'Here's a young woman who isn't being challenged. Here's a young woman who might need to talk.'"

Then he put his hand on my shoulder in a way that was intended to be fatherly, but Dad and I have a standing *no physical contact* policy.

"You can tell me anything, Astrid," he said, motioning around his office. "This is a safe space. You can't get in trouble for anything you do or say here."

He had an empty vase on the side of his desk. It was glass with flowers painted on the side. I walked over and knocked it to the ground and watched as it shattered.

"Safe space," I said. And then I left.

After that, we didn't pretend to be friends. We both pretty much hated each other, and that was perfectly fine with me. I didn't have friends at Bristol; most people left me alone. Instead, I had accomplices. This isn't to imply that I had this crack team of genius spies like in movies. I didn't, but they usually did a good job. The group consisted of Pierre, Peter and Jeremy Elfrish, Maribelle Rohit, Joe Flemming, and Talia Pasteur—all skilled in different ways, all willing to help me for a price. They were loyal—at least I thought they were. Accomplices are like friends, only they don't care about you. They care about stuff—money, grades, boyfriends, alcohol, or whatever.

Me, I wanted power. My grandfather liked to say, "You know power is the best thing in the world because as soon as you have it, everyone is trying to take it from you." No one is ever trying to take your friends away, so that's how you know they're less important.

I bribed a janitor during my freshman year for a master key to every door on campus, which I kept with me almost all the time until it disappeared from my room during junior year. With that key, I could go anywhere, but pretty soon, I could go anywhere anyway. Everyone was a little scared of me. As the years passed, I developed a kind of reputation.

When I walked into chapel the first day of senior year, someone was in my seat. All it took was a sideways glance, and that girl ran. She actually ran. She didn't have anything to worry about, though. I'm not a bully. I don't mess with the weak. I take people down who need to be taken down.

A few days after that, someone took me down. Someone betrayed me and I left.

I wasn't expecting to be back so soon. But as I walked into the administration building, the front left window still broken from the day before my expulsion, I thought about something my sister Lisbet would often say: "Every door is a window." She was trying to say *Every time a door closes, a window opens,* but she remembered it wrong. I liked it though. It meant that every moment can be an opportunity and that's something I believe. If I played it right with Dean Rein it was possible I could just hit reset on the past week, return to Bristol, and never have to spend one minute in Cadorette Township High School, the local public school. I was practically smiling at the thought when I walked into Dean Rein's office. Dean Rein didn't look all that happy to be sitting there with me, though, which was weird because it was his stupid idea to be my therapist in the first place.

"Isn't this unethical?" I asked when I sat down in his office.

"Why is that, Astrid?"

"This doesn't seem kosher at all. You know me. Aren't you not allowed to be the psychologist of someone you know? I mean, I don't even know if you're a real doctor."

"Before teaching, I did this as a profession. And I keep my license current. You are no longer one of my students, so it's not unethical. And yes, I am a real doctor."

He pointed to a wall of framed diplomas. I wondered if anyone had ever closely looked at that wall. There were way more diplomas than he could've possibly earned. Nobody could go to that many schools. Eventually, I realized that some of the documents weren't even diplomas.

They were more like certificates. One of them said that he was Camper of the Week at something called Happy Time Day Camp in 1961.

"Well, not a real doctor," I pointed out. "A PhD isn't a real doctor."

"A PhD is very much a real doctor." He pursed his lips together.

"My cousin Gretchen has a PhD in Performance Studies. I went to her to get my appendix taken out, and you know what happened?"

He rolled his eyes. "What happened, Astrid?"

"I died." I stood up and peered more closely at the diplomas. I swear, some of the important words looked glued on. "Johns Hopkins? That sounds made up."

"It isn't made up. It's a fine institution."

"If it's a real place, is Johns Hopkins a guy or is it two guys? You know, like Larry Johns and Bill Hopkins. And they started up the college together."

"I don't know, Astrid, I think it's one person. Can you—?"

"There's one person and his first name is 'Johns'? That's, like, the stupidest thing I ever heard. His name is plural. I bet he thought that made him sound really important. 'I am two Johns in one.'"

"Could you—?"

"You know what I'm going to name my kid?"

"Honestly, it doesn't—"

"When I have a kid, I want her to be really important, so her name has to be really plural. I'm going to name her Childrens."

He looked at me like I was speaking a different language. "Children?"

"Not 'Children.' Childrens. Childrens Krieger."

"So, you'd like to have a child someday, Astrid?"

"I'd like to have Childrens. Childrens Krieger. Are you even listening to me? You should really take a better look at that diploma. It really looks fake."

He turned his head a little to look, but he noticed me watching him, and he stopped. "I'm not going to look at my diploma. I know what it says. And we're here to talk about you, not me."

"Fine."

"Fine."

He took a deep, careful breath and looked down at his legal pad. "Why do *you* think you're here?"

"You know why I'm here."

Dean Rein was skinny and shaped like a damp sock. Every time he moved his arm, his entire torso seemed to seep into the floor. When he first came to Bristol, he addressed the school in chapel and said something like,

"My heart has always been in education." The truth of his change in career is a little more complicated. His son, Martin Jr., was making meth, and he blew his arm clean off in the Rein garage. Somehow the experience made Dean Rein take a look at his life and decide that he should take a more active role in shaping the lives of young people. Not his son, mind you. Other young people whom he didn't know. He told me once that I reminded him of his son, though I imagine not in the sense that I'm a girl and have the amount of hands needed to clap.

"What I'm asking is, why has your life brought you to this place? Why do you think your parents and I felt you needed to make changes?"

"I was expelled."

"And why did that happen?" he said.

"Because someone betrayed me, and then you expelled me."

"I feel like we're going in circles. You broke our honor code at Bristol. We are firmly against cheating. I caught you cheating. You were expelled. The end."

"Who set me up, Dean Rein?"

"Do we need to go into this again?"

My silence told him that yeah, we did.

"This is supposed to be therapy," he said.

"I find the tale of my own downfall therapeutic."

"Do you really, or is this just an excuse to have another argument with me about your expulsion?"

"I find arguing with you therapeutic too."

He sighed and opened a drawer and took out a folder and from that, a list of names. "Listen, Astrid, this is very simple. Here's a list of the students whom I called into my office last week: Peter and Jeremy Elfrish. Maribelle Rohit. Joe Flemming. Talia Pasteur. Do those names sound familiar to you?"

I shrugged.

"Luk az burrssszz," he said, as if that was an answer that would explain everything instead of what it sounded like to me, a jumble of meaningless sounds.

"'Look as bur az?'" I repeated to make sure I heard him correctly.

Dean Rein pointed to the list of names. And there on the bottom—*Lukas Borsz.*

"Do you know Lukas Borsz, Astrid?"

"No."

"Sure you do. Tall, blond. The lacrosse team. He's from the Czech Republic. He's with you all the time. Come on, jog that memory of yours."

"You mean Pierre?"

Dean Rein didn't say anything, which I took as a yes. "I'm not going to give him the pleasure of me remembering his real name," I said. "I call him Pierre. Probably because his name is *Look as bur az*. That sure doesn't roll off the tongue."

"Lukas . . . *Pierre* . . . we had a long conversation the day before you had to leave our school."

"Did Pierre read you one of his poems? They're horrible, aren't they? 'Flowers' doesn't *rhyme* with 'flowers.' They're the same—"

"I didn't have an agenda. I didn't even mention your name."

"Then why did you bring *those* people in?"

"I'm observant, Astrid. I'd been watching you for a long time. I watched whom you interacted with. They each came in, and I just brought up a few things. Tests. Term papers. Cheating. Things like that. Lukas and the others, they all had a lot to say."

"I'll bet they did. Because they all cheated in your class."

"Funny. They all said it was you. Only you."

"I'm sure they would. Did they have proof?"

"No," Dean Rein said, fiddling with some paper in his manila folder. "They didn't need it. In the mail I received some papers. Blank tests. From every year you were at Bristol. An advance copy of every test you ever took at Bristol."

"They're old tests. There's nothing against the rules about having tests that I already took."

He flipped to the last paper. "This test is the midterm to my senior Psychology class. I'm not giving it for three weeks."

"This doesn't prove anything. Anyone could've had these."

"No student has the exact same schedule. Different English classes, different years. Some take Art History. Some take Music Appreciation. Over several years, your schedule is a thumbprint. These tests match your class schedule. Only your schedule. How would you explain this phenomenon?"

"You know that theory about how if an infinite number of monkeys typed on an infinite number of typewriters, they'd eventually write the complete works of William Shakespeare?"

"So in this scenario, are you Shakespeare or the monkeys?"

I thought about it for a second. "The monkeys, sir."

"You're a real firecracker, Astrid, aren't you?" *Firecracker* is what people in certain social circles say when what they really mean is *asshole*.

"Thank you," I said. "Have I mentioned your head is shaped like an actual penis?"

"Yes you have. On a few occasions." He sighed. "I was hoping perhaps I made a mistake. You didn't cheat. I brought in each of your friends and on some level, I hoped they would defend you. That they would find a hole in my logic. But your friends all sold you out, Ms. Krieger."

"They're not my friends."

"No, I guess they're not. Girl like you, you don't have any real friends, do you?"

"I did the work, sir," I lied.

"Are you lying?"

"No, I'm not lying," I said, also lying.

"Can you prove it?"

"How would you like me to prove it, sir?"

"Tell me the name of one of the books that you read in Introduction to Psychology. If you were set up, you should be able to tell me that much."

I couldn't think of anything. I mean, I brought a note-book to class, but I could hardly say the name of a book for his class was *Notebook*. He was talking about the thick blue textbook he passed out on the first day last year. It had a lightbulb on the cover and I remembered that because I thought it was the stupidest thing in the world. Like, psychology is supposed to be a real serious thing but the ideas in the book should be taken exactly as seriously as when Wile E. Coyote has a plan. At that moment,

I knew exactly where that book was. It was under a pair of yellow pants that I never wore. They were probably Lisbet's. Lisbet would probably think yellow pants were a great thing to own. I still had no idea what the book was called.

"No, I understand. That's a difficult question," he said. "You've only taken Introduction to Psychology for about a year. How about any book you've read in your three years at this school? Any one will do." And then he let himself smile a little.

I always had a backup plan. If something was going in a direction I didn't like, I had a way of pulling it back. Usually my backup plans involved money. Money isn't always the cleverest solution to a problem, but it works almost every time. But Dean Rein knew I had money. He knew that if he wanted a building or a squash court in exchange for another free pass for me, he would've never expelled me at all. In fact, there already was a building and a squash court paid for by an endowment from the Krieger family expressly for this purpose. He wasn't blinking. He wasn't flinching. And I had no answer to his stupid question. For once, I had no backup plan.

"You know," I said. "People who do the work—*like me*—can't always remember what the books were c—"

"*Introduction to Psychology.*"

"Huh?"

"The textbook for your introductory psychology class is called *Introduction to Psychology*."

"So it is." I nodded sagely, as if I'd known all along. "You know, I'm not sentimental. I'm also not an idiot. If I did cheat, which I didn't, I swear," I lied, "why would I keep those old tests knowing that someone could send them to you at some point? That doesn't even make sense."

"Maybe"—Dean Rein leaned back in his chair—"you wanted to get caught. It's like I said when you first came into my office those years ago; maybe you just wanted to talk."

"Ugh."

"In these sessions, I'd like to take you out of your comfort zone, okay? I'm interested in some real honesty from you. Here's a question, an idea I've been playing around with for you . . . have you ever really done something that you didn't want to do?"

"Why would I?"

"What I mean is have you done something that someone else wants you to do or something that would make someone else happy?"

"I'm not following you."

"Like help a friend move, or volunteer at a charity, or visit a family member in the hospital?"

I didn't say anything. I just blinked a few times.

"I have an assignment for you," he continued.

"Homework? I don't even go to this school anymore."

"This is the process. It's an exercise. I want you to really think about how you make your decisions and why. So, make a list this week of at least three things that you did even though you didn't want to."

"I can do it right now." It was easy. I finished it in my mind almost instantly. I wrote it on his legal pad and handed him back the list.

"Why would you draw a picture of my underwear?" he said.

"I didn't want to. That's the point, right?"

"None of these things count," he said.

"Why doesn't it count?"

"Because it's my assignment and I make the rules. I'm not talking about bathroom stuff, Astrid. I'm talking about actual things you do even though you don't want to. Nice things for other people."

"Fine."

"Write the assignment down."

"I'll write it on my hand."

I wrote DO 3 THINGS I DON'T WANT TO DO, [SOMETHING SOMETHING].

He seemed relatively satisfied, which wasn't my intention at all.

"What happens if I don't do the assignment?" I said.

"It's your time. It's your life. Maybe I don't even care what you do."

## RECORD OF ARREST
### Southboro Police Department, Southboro, CT

**KRIEGER, ASTRID J.**

**Known Alias(es):** Astrid Cooper, Allison Krieger, Michelle Regularperson, Yves Graneveis, Killer D. Dog, Wednesday Mustacheface.

**Address:** The Bristol Academy, 1134 Bristol Dr., Southboro

**Hair color:** Brown      **Eye color:** Blue

**Height:** 5'2"      **Weight:** 104

**Age as of current date (if minor, write MINOR):** MINOR (age 17)

**ARRESTS (MOST RECENT FIRST) AND ARREST LOCATION**

· Armed robbery with a dangerous weapon (pepper spray)— Lulu's Gas and Snacks

· Resisting arrest (and also insulting the arresting officer's mother, which is not against the law but should be noted)

· Conspiracy to hire airplane to skywrite curse words over the town square on Christmas Eve. (Further investigation concluded that this breaks no actual laws, though the city council asks that a record of the act be included.)—Southboro Town Square

· Selling city property without permission. (The perpetrator does not and has not ever had authorization to sell rights to the Southboro Police Department's name and facilities to the People's Republic of China.)—Southboro Police Department

· Making a false police report. (Evidence proved that there have never been "orphan auctions" in the basement of the Southboro Police Department.)—Southboro Police Department

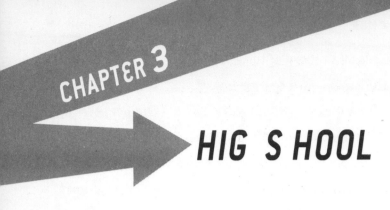

# CHAPTER 3

# HIG S HOOL

**I**t was warm out. Much warmer when I left Dean Rein's office than it had been an hour before. I wore a big white coat so no one would see me, and it felt like a mistake. My arms felt sticky. My hair was curling into damp little brown nests, one of which kept bouncing against my forehead and dripping into my eye.

I stuck one of my hands into my bag in search of gum, and my other hand just dangled around like a noodle. I looked at the thing I wrote on my palm—the thing about doing three things. It couldn't really be hard. How could it? Because if it *was* too hard, I wasn't going to do it. I didn't like doing things that were very hard.

My driver was circling around campus. There aren't really streets for parking at Bristol. Sometimes kids ride horses, and the administration doesn't like cars to be mingling with the horses. Bristol cared a lot about appearances and horses. You can't have too many pictures of stupid horses. I suddenly wished I knew how to drive. I took off the jacket and held it in my arm. I was no longer invisible. The whole world could see me. But only one person actually did.

"You look so terrible," she said.

I turned around. I had no idea who was talking to me. There was a girl standing right there, but she didn't look like anyone I'd ever seen before. She had this brutally short, almost-white hair and red, red lips. She was either wearing ultra-heavy eye makeup or someone had recently punched her twice in the face with perfectly circular fists.

"I used to think you were the most beautiful girl I'd ever seen, you know? I hated you for that," she commented. "What are you even doing here?"

I wasn't thunderstruck. I could think at the same steady rate I always did. I had plenty of things I could say back to this person, but I couldn't quite figure out what my goal was. If I was thinking of a comeback, I would have to solve two mysteries at the same time. Unfortunately, I was too preoccupied with the more important mystery: figuring out who would be so stupid as to say that I looked terrible right to my face. She was liable to lose a finger. *And do I look terrible?* I found myself wondering. I was usually happy with how I looked and I couldn't imagine I had changed that afternoon. I rubbed the sides of my face from the sharp point of my chin, up my cheekbones, and across my forehead to the little old scar above the bridge of my nose. Lisbet once said that people would murder for my eyebrows—which is *not* the perfect crime—but as I ran my fingers along them, they were still as they always were—pointed in their perpetual "are you fucking kidding me" arch.

"Say something." She laughed a little bit. Fearless. "Superman lost her cape, huh?"

And then I figured out who she was. Her laugh gave her away. This was Talia Pasteur. She was a member of the group of names Dean Rein read off in his office. But Talia wasn't just anyone on the list. She was my right hand. I probably trusted her the most. And the person you trust most will always be the first person to let you down. "Didn't you used to have braces, Talia?"

"I had a lot taken off, Astrid. A lot." And she was not exaggerating. I'm actually surprised I recognized her as Talia at all. She had taken many steps in the past week.

"That's not how Superman works, by the way," I told her. "Superman doesn't get his powers from his cape, so—"

"I don't have any idea how Superman works," Talia snapped. "I don't read comic books."

"I don't read comic books either. But it's just something everyone knows."

"But you're no longer one to tell people what they should or shouldn't know, are you?" Talia asked smugly.

Talia and I were never exactly friends, but she was *almost* there. I kind of liked her. I rarely thought about her. When I was at Bristol, I needed to have people around me who had particular talents I could use. And Talia Pasteur's talent? Well, she always said yes, she didn't ask a lot of questions, and she looked like a tree.

I'm not kidding about that. Talia Pasteur's most practical skill was camouflage. When I first saw her the year before, it was the first thing I noticed about her. Maybe someone else would notice her tiny eyes or her way of touching people every time she said anything. If she was ordering coffee and needed extra milk, she would touch the coffee guy's arm, lean in, and speak in a quiet voice as if the extra milk transaction was a special secret the two of them shared.

But that's not what I noticed. It's why I'm different. I can see someone's value in a way others can't. I noticed the way her frizzy hair whirled around her head like an assortment of twigs and the way her baggy brown sweater made her look lumpier than she was underneath, and I could picture her among a field of trees. I often thought about how she would be virtually indistinguishable in that field. You could walk right by her and figure her for a little spruce. She could hide almost anywhere. She could run surveillance. She was useful. Of course, she didn't look like a tree anymore. In addition to her haircut and weird makeup, she had this short dress that could also be a long shirt. She was wearing tights as pants. Tights are not pants. She followed a straight path when she walked, completely unconcerned by the people in her way. Two boys actually jumped because she wasn't changing course. Talia had never been mean before. I remembered her being nice, even though I never did anything around her to inspire kindness. But whatever she was—that person was somehow gone. And I thought about the circumstances of my getting kicked out of Bristol. And I thought about how I got set up. The night before I was expelled, Talia and I broke into the administrative building. She even threw the brick. I wondered whether Talia might have had some additional skills beyond resembling shrubbery. She might have had a lot of things rolling around in that head of hers.

As I was walking away, I heard Talia yell after me. "Hey Astrid, enjoy your new school." She didn't mean it.

>>>>>>>>>>>>

When I think back to my first day of public school, I remember most clearly this burning feeling that started in my chest and moved to the top of my head and then down again. It wasn't anger. That's a hot feeling too, but it's different. With anger, it's like you're breathing fire and you have to just unleash the flames at whoever is around you. Being angry is like being a dragon. This was more like a fever, one that didn't come with aches or the chills. But it still made me want to crawl back into bed that morning. I probably could have. It had been ten days since my parents told me I had to go to Cadorette Township High School. I bought myself a few days while I went to Bristol to see Dean Rein, and then I had to wait for Bristol to send over my transcripts. And then I just didn't go for a few days. I knew it didn't matter to my parents enough to, like, check to make sure I actually was there.

I spent a lot of those ten days in my grandfather's study. It was a room with oak walls and oak furniture and leather-bound books that no one ever read. Some of them were in Latin. I knew that my grandfather didn't understand Latin (who does?); he just liked them there. They were important books, and he was a decidedly important man, so it was fitting. On the walls were pictures of his life and other important people. Framed above his desk was a black-and-white photo of my grandfather during World War II with his arm around John F. Kennedy. Kennedy wrote *Monty, Go fuck yourself! Jack*. They were friends, I think. Kennedy was actually the guy who shot my grandfather in the kidney. It was during a game of Russian roulette in the middle of the Pacific Ocean.

At the end of the day, after my grandfather's bosomy nurse would go wherever it was she went, my grandfather would sit in the study with me. He was only allowed to smoke a cigar once a day, so usually the cigar in his mouth would be unlit, even though he pretended it was doing the thing cigars do. He stared long at an engraving of a giant whale in an old book, as if it was telling him something. "How long are you going to hide out here?" he asked.

"Until I'm old and wrinkly and useless," I said. "Like you."

He smiled but then closed his book with a thud. "It's time," he said. "It's time to go."

Then the burning started all over again.

>>>>>>>>>>>>

The public school was brick with yellow aluminum siding. There were hundreds of paint strokes in different yellowy colors all over the building. It must have been to cover up graffiti, but plenty of new graffiti had popped up since the last time they painted. There was a drawing of boobs and some squiggly letters that may have said *Paul* or *Fuego* or anything in between. There were small metal letters to the left of the front door that said *Cadorette Township Hig S hool*. An *h* and a *c* were missing. In order to distract myself, I invented several fictional suspects for the stolen letters (Heather Carter, Henry Chatwick, Hugo Carboncini), but my temperature wasn't going down. I saw people walk into the school around me, avoiding contact like I was a broken slab of sidewalk surrounded by orange cones, a potential safety hazard.

The dress I wore that day was also keeping a wide circle open around me. I wore a uniform at Bristol, so all my regular clothes were mostly these complicated outfits for formal occasions. The dress wasn't long, but it was as wide as my outstretched arms. It was from Denmark, and they make weird dresses in Denmark. No one else walking past me was wearing a dress. Or even a skirt. Not one person. The girls wore jeans. Most were very tight. Some of the boys wore shorts with basketball teams on them, but most of them also wore jeans. I had never owned a pair of jeans, and I didn't plan on it. I am not a cowboy, a farmer, or a 1950s greaser. I just don't really get it.

"What are you looking at, princess?" The person addressing me said it in a singsong voice that made it clear he was sharing a joke that I wasn't involved in. And even though he asked me what I was looking at, he didn't wait around for my answer. He just laughed and punched his friend on the arm. People punched their friends on the arm a lot in public school.

There were no longer people walking through the front entrance. The yellow buses parked outside had begun driving away. It was now or never, so I walked inside.

I was hit with the smell of glue and urine. Magazines and hamburgers. It was in the walls, the sort of smell that never leaves.

>>>>>>>>>>>>

"Your first day, and you're late," the bearded man stated.

This was the principal, Mr. Barth. When he told me his name, I said, "The kids must have a lot of names for you."

"And they'll have a lot of names for you too, Astrid," he said, quickly dodging the filing cabinets and the myriad of secretaries that decorated the room, dropping a paper in an in-box, and signing a form in triplicate. His beard was possibly his most distinguishing trait; it was long and thick, as though it had been with him since he could grow one. He was likely into the Grateful Dead. The thing about the beard was that it was half full of white hairs. And he was plump, so as soon as the white hairs became the majority, he would no longer be a hippie. He would be Santa Claus. I had the feeling that this shift of balance between white and brown could happen at any moment, possibly by Christmas.

"The students will be pretty excited to have you here. We've never had a celebrity student."

"I'm not a celebrity."

"Yeah, but you're a celebrity for Cadorette. You're notorious."

"Hardly."

"I was sent your arrest record when you enrolled."

"That doesn't seem like the sort of thing that's allowed to get out."

"It's exactly the sort of thing that's allowed to get out," he said. "I kind of require it. The secret service called me as well."

"You bring one knife to a White House state dinner . . . When did the world lose its sense of humor?"

"I don't know. It was gradual. Everyone here knows who you are, I'm sure."

I rolled my eyes. "Perfect."

"Do you have Astrid's schedule, Mrs. Ramos?" Mr. Barth asked one of the women typing on an ancient computer. She tore a piece of paper out of a printer—the kind of printer that makes a screeching sound as it prints. It may have been fifty years old.

"I can get you a map, but I don't think you'll need it," Mr. Barth said as he pointed to a series of numbers and letters on the schedule. "This is A hall. The parallel hall is D hall. So then that's B and that's C. And if there's a 2 in the room number, it's on the second floor. The cafeteria, well, you won't miss that. Or the gym. Does that make sense to you?"

"Does it make sense to you?" I asked. He was already back by a filing cabinet and in the middle of asking the other secretary about an in-service day. He seemingly had no further interest in me, which was refreshing. But it also left me with no idea whether or not I was supposed to stand there or leave.

"Do I need to get you a guide?" he asked in a tone that could've been genuine or could've been another *What are you looking at, princess?*

"I'll be fine. A hall, D hall, something, something. Upstairs, something, something. Great. See you at graduation."

"Mrs. Ramos, could you page, um . . . " He looked at the schedule in my hand. "Lucy Redlich's in her English class. Page her, would you? Lucy Redlich will show you around, Astrid. This is old hat for her. We've had a lot of transfers this week."

"Is that normal?" I said.

"No. Not at all." And again, Mr. Barth buried his head in a filing cabinet.

>>>>>>>>>>>>>

You could probably guess exactly what Lucy Redlich was like. I think it's universal that the girl who is the principal's go-to for showing people around for no personal gain is rarely the sort who attracts other people. Lucy was covered in freckles and ate her own hair. She munched on that stuff like it was dinner. It was disgusting. I'm getting a little queasy just thinking about it right now.

"I'm really happy to meet you," she said. And I think she meant it, though I don't know why. She had this horrible lisp. It was so bad that instead of "Lucy Redlich," she called herself "Lucy Wet Lick."

"Did you do plays or student government or marching band at your old school?" she asked.

"No."

"Forensics or FFA or DECA?"

"I don't have the faintest idea what you're talking about."

"Did they assign you a locker?"

"That's a real thing?" And then I realized I was surrounded by lockers. Every spare inch of wall space had lockers. I guess you probably think it's ridiculous that I was surprised, but I seriously thought lockers were just props they used in movies about high schools. I didn't think that people actually used them anymore. Why would kids need all that storage? We weren't settling in for a long weekend. I worried for a second that I wouldn't get to leave.

Lucy laughed, but I could tell she wasn't laughing at me. Even when she laughed, there was still a chunk of hair in her mouth. She sounded like a horse choking on hay.

She looked again at my schedule and pointed to a series of numbers. "That's your locker number. That's your combination."

"I'm not going to remember that," I told her. And I never did.

She laughed again and chomped and stopped outside a classroom door. "You're going to just love it here," she said, staring with a smile at a loose piece of the ceiling.

"I don't think I will."

"You just have to meet people. Everyone's really nice." She again gazed absently toward the fluorescent lights. It was a little odd that she thought everyone was nice. Because I'd been there for, like, two minutes, and I was pretty sure no one was nice. She stuck her hand into her bag and rummaged around in there until she found what she was looking for. She pulled out an envelope and handed it to me shyly. "I invited everybody I know to my birthday. That'll be a good place to meet people, I think," she said.

I looked at the envelope suspiciously, like it was going to blow up. I'd never been invited to a birthday party before, at least never to one that didn't end with a Brunei prince shooting an endangered condor with a gold revolver off the side of a 450-foot-yacht. Regular birthdays had never sounded like occasions I would want to attend anyway. Besides all that, Lucy seemed too old to be having a birthday party. I was almost positive she wasn't six.

"Just RSVP by the end of the week," she said.

"Oh. I can't come."

"You don't even know when it is," she said.

"Still. I'm sure I have something else."

"It's going to be fun."

"Will there be a magician?"

Lucy smiled. "Maybe."

"Then I for sure won't be there."

Lucy found me entertaining rather than convincing. I stuffed the invitation deep into my pocket. I did not want to go to Lucy Redlich's birthday party. But then I remembered Dean Rein's challenge. I was supposed to do things I didn't want to do. Maybe Lucy's party would be my first thing. Lucy opened a door on our right and walked in with a smile. I noticed that nobody smiled back or even looked at her. "This is our English class," she told me.

Before I'd even stepped inside the classroom, I heard something I didn't like at all. It was ominous—the kind of sound that, had I been starring in a horror movie, would have been preceded by violins shrieking and then drums banging. And then a second later I would be dead.

The sound was a voice. "I believe my eyes are deceiving me," the voice said. The voice was mind-boggling. It formed a soup of words that didn't really sound like what they were supposed to. I was in a different school and a different town, yet Pierre was right behind me.

A POEM FOR ASTRID

The Window
By Lukas Borsz

Sometimes at night I look through the window,
At night,
Through my window.
And I see a wisp of you moving through the snow.
I smile,
Every night,

46

When I see you,

Through my window.

My head is full of birds,

They sing their song.

My heart flows with *štěstí* (that is the Czech word for "happiness"),

And it sings its song.

And then across the way,

I can see your window,

And I wonder what you think,

At night,

Through your window,

When you look down,

And see me.

# CHAPTER 4

# A BOOK THAT CHANGED MY LIFE

If you were to ask Pierre who he is to me, the first thing he would probably say is, "My name's not Pierre." And while that's true, if you saw a blond guy wearing a tracksuit talking on a neon green cell phone with a big stupid grin on his face all the time and a very phlegmy accent, I'm positive you would know who I was talking about if I called that guy Pierre.

The second thing Pierre would say is that he's my boyfriend. I'm not positive how he got that idea, but he's held onto it for a long time, and I've had a hard time getting rid of him. We've kissed a few times (because I needed some furniture moved), but beyond that, I'd never held his hand or encouraged any of the big stupid European things he does to show me how he feels. He buys me a lot of flowers. I have no use for flowers. Flowers die before they do anything. If someone wants to win me over, they should give me something useful, like juice boxes or a boat.

Even if Pierre was my boyfriend, he ended up not being a very good one. He was one of the people who told Dean Rein I'd cheated. Needless to say, I was not very happy to see him standing behind me in the doorway of my classroom at Cadorette.

Pierre looked completely ridiculous. Every article of clothing had giant words across it. He clearly had no idea what was meant for boys and what was meant for girls and what people stopped wearing about ten years ago. His giant shirt said *Democracy* and featured a snake weaving through a flaming skull. His jacket was a pattern of spiderwebs and flannel and zigzags and colored squares. His sweatpants said *smack it* across the butt.

"I had a baseball hat," Pierre said. "But they wouldn't let me wear it because there is a dress code. You can hide weapons in a baseball hat. Can you believe it?"

"What are you doing in my English class, Pierre?"

"I should ask you the same question, Astrid. I have been in this class for a week."

"No you shouldn't because it's *my* English class. You don't even speak English."

"I've been in this country for five years. I'm speaking English right now."

I folded my arms across my chest. "You have to leave."

"No, I cannot. There was nothing left for me at Bristol.

Without you, my heart was a rowboat without the row. Understand?"

"Barely."

"I am heartbroken with how things ended with us at Bristol."

"You sold me out. You *told* on me."

"Don't hate me," Pierre said. "I was dazzled by numbers and percentages. I had no choice but to name names."

"I would never have done that to you."

"You have done that to me."

"I would never do it again. Bloods protect Bloods."

"What is this Bloods?"

"Forget it," I said.

Pierre made what I called his "Shakespeare face." It's when he gets really serious and puts his nose in the air like he's a character in a Shakespeare play. "Does this mean that we are breaking up?" he asked.

"I wasn't aware that we were together."

"I love you, Astrid," Shakespeare Face said.

I had no idea what I was supposed to say back to him. I didn't love him. Not even a little bit. I would have no problem lying to him if I thought there was anything much to gain from it, but there wasn't. Uttering those words would hurt me a lot more than they would help. He would surround me with his arms and lean close to my mouth so I could get sick from his cologne, which smelled like peach schnapps and gunpowder. I didn't want him to touch me. I didn't want his face against mine. The few times we kissed in the past, his tongue had bounced around like a dying slug in my mouth. I could taste him on me for weeks after, no matter how much I brushed my teeth. What had he been eating? Fried chicken? Onions? Old shoes?

I walked into the classroom. Lucy Wet Lick pointed to an empty seat next to her. Predictably, it was in the front row. In another predictable maneuver, Pierre took the seat next to me. And everyone else in the class just stared at me, because of course.

"I think you have to live in the town to go to the public school. I live in Cadorette. I'm sure there are schools for you in . . . Bulgaria," I said to Pierre.

"Czech Republic. They made an exception for me because I am a conduit to the international world." Pierre leaned in quietly. "And I also said I would find out who is dealing cocaine." He pointed to a nervous kid in the back row. "I think I will say it is that one. He seems to fidget."

Ms. Sharp was a young teacher. A few weeks before, she'd been full of ambition. A few months before that, she was still the president of her sorority. By the time I was in the class, she had become a pale and terrified shadow of her former self.

She wrote in weak script on the chalkboard until the chalk broke in her hand and crumbled to the floor. The board read *Oral Reports*, and even before anyone laughed, she quietly said, "*Enough*. Just enough already." She glanced at a piece of paper that lay on her desk and jotted something in a notebook with a felt-tip pen. "It's just an embarrassment of riches this week. Another new transfer. Pretty soon this whole class will be full of new students who haven't read the book." She seemed exasperated and out of breath. "Krieger., A., do you want to come up here and introduce yourself?"

I did not want to. I wanted to fling my bag across the room, leave, and never return. I felt a scalding heat all over my face. My legs shook with nervous energy. My hand was clean now, but I remembered what I had written on it days before: DO THINGS I DON'T WANT TO DO. Standing up in class wasn't like me at all, but I didn't feel like me either. I stood up. I could feel everyone looking at me. I let myself focus on a few of their faces and got mostly confused looks in return. A girl with long hair, a shirt that showed off her entire abdomen, and a lazy eye laughed and glanced around at the others, eager to share her amusement.

The only person who wasn't just gawking at me was sitting two seats away from mine in the first row. He had this messy hair like he'd just climbed out of bed, but I suspected he'd put in some effort to get it that way. He wore a blue-and-white polyester shirt that looked exactly like this thing my dad wore in some notorious pictures from the seventies that chronicled a period he referred to as his "Lost Weekend."

The polyester kid was sitting in the class like it was the most relaxing thing in the whole world. He stretched out his legs, resting his red-sneakered feet directly in front of me. He glared over his shoulder at the rest of the class, holding a finger to his lips to quiet them.

He wasn't threatening at all. No one seemed to care. A few guys loudly mocked his "Shhhh." I guess it must've been very frustrating for everyone to look at his clothes and not know what his favorite basketball team was. I can't really explain it, but I didn't feel that same nervous, hot, leg-shaking feeling when I looked at that kid who was now right in front of me.

"Why don't you tell us your name?" Ms. Sharp said.

"Okay. I'm Astrid Krieger."

"Why hello, ASS-trid." This was from a big guy with a red face and a T-shirt that said *Buttwiser, King of Rears*. From that day forward I almost never saw that guy wearing anything that didn't say something good about beer, bad about girls, or speculate about who farted. He will probably be married in a shirt that says *Don't worry, she'll look good after a six-pack*.

A few kids laughed. Beer Shirt nodded, accepting the admiration as if he'd been the first to think of this particular play on words. And believe it or not, it was the first time I'd heard it. No one had ever been bold enough or stupid enough to make fun of me before. And I'd never thought too much about the ways in which my name sounded like a body part. I paused for a second to think about whether or not Krieger also sounded like something bad. It didn't. Meager. Eager. Nah.

"Doug!" Ms. Sharp yelled. Doug. Lug. Fug. Rug. Mug. Jug. Tug. Nope, nothing great. I would work on it. "Go on, Astrid."

"Okay," I said, "I just transferred here from Bristol, which is a school just like this one, except it's kind of nicer. But I'm just, you know, a regular girl like anyone else. Um, I enjoy music and hanging out and status updating and whatever you people do. Oh, and I live in a rocket ship. But it's just a prototype, so it doesn't work."

"Neat." Ms. Sharp nodded. "And why don't you tell the class about a book that changed your life."

I hadn't yet written the book you're reading right now, so I didn't really have anything much to say. Only one book at that point had particularly changed my life, and that was *Introduction to Psychology*. But those words didn't come out. I mean, that's what I tried to say, but it came out as, "Neener durrm maaaaaa—" That was weird. It surprised the hell out of me. I looked right at all those faces, smiling and laughing. These people. This place. My face was feeling hot again. My legs shook more. And then I looked at the ceiling. There was a spitball that may have been sixty years old hanging there. And then I remember thinking, *Why am I looking at the ceiling?* But it was too late. It was all blurry. My legs decided that they were no longer interested in holding my body up, which is total bullshit because they have *one job*. And then I fell. I fainted. I actually fainted for real. *Boom.* My head fell right into a piece of wood. *Smack.* And it was loud, and it hurt, and that's all I remember.

# CHAPTER 5

# THANKS FOR THE INFORMATION, EINSTEIN

**W**hen I was ten years old, the Kriegers went to Paris. It wasn't exactly a vacation. My grandfather and father had a meeting with some Saudi Arabians in the restaurant at the George V hotel. One morning, I was supposed to stay in the room but found myself getting incredibly bored. Vivi was sorting through piles of clothes, and Lisbet was seated in a plush velvet chair, enamored of the pigeons outside the east sitting room window. I couldn't take it anymore, so I snuck out. I say "snuck out," but I actually just opened the door and left. No one even noticed. I wandered over to the restaurant in search of my grandfather. I'm hazy about what was actually happening there. In my imagination, one of the Saudis was negotiating to purchase Lisbet, but that was probably just wishful thinking. I knew I wasn't supposed to be there, and after the whole incident was over, I was sworn to secrecy. (I mention it now because the non-Kriegers who were involved are no longer alive.)

I hovered around the maitre d' podium for a little bit, slowly inching closer to the table where my grandfather and the others sat. "What is it, Puppy?" he asked when he finally made eye contact.

"I've been in the room all day. It's horrible."

He wasn't mad. He just smiled. "How about you handle the rest of the day, Dirk?" he said to my father, who started breathing heavily from the shock of it. Grandpa got up and took my hand. "Let's get our butts the hell out of here. It's boring to me, so I can only imagine what it's like for you."

We started walking fast—practically running. He was old even then, but he could outrun pretty much anyone. We went through a gate and past a length of tourists, and then we stopped. "Here we are," he said.

"This is a museum. If I wanted to be bored, I could've stayed in the hotel with Lisbet."

"This isn't a museum, Monkey. It's the mother-fucking Louvre." He pronounced it *Loov-er* because he refused to speak any French.

"Yeah, I can see that."

"Don't worry. I didn't take you here to learn about art. I'm trying to stay awake too. But I am going to teach you something."

"Well, that's just great."

He pulled my arm and we moved past the line. I don't know if he got special treatment or something, but no one stopped him. He looked like he knew what he was doing. We moved into these long hallways full of paintings. People were shoving their way over to the *Mona Lisa* like they expected her to do something other than be a painting, and Grandpa and I laughed a little before we moved on.

"I want you to find your painting," he said.

"What do you mean?"

"There's a ton of paintings here. I want you to find yours. You'll know it when you see it."

I kind of had no idea what he was talking about, but I looked around quickly as we walked through. Most of the stuff was about Jesus or wars or Jesus in wars or ladies taking baths, and I didn't really care for any of it. But then we crossed into another room, and I understood what he was talking about. I'd seen a painting of this girl. She was smiling mischievously, like she knew she'd done something wrong or was secretly teasing someone. She wore a boa that moved around her like a snake and her hands were encased in long, golden gloves.

"Well, I'll be. It's like you're looking in a mirror, huh?" Grandpa said.

"Kind of. I guess. Is that what you meant? Is that my painting?"

"There's only one way to find out, isn't there?" I wasn't sure where he was going with it, and he seemed a little bothered that I wasn't catching on. "Take it," he said.

"Huh?"

"I sure as hell know I'm not speaking French. You heard me. Take it. It's your painting."

He wasn't smiling, so it seemed like this wasn't a joke. In fact, he was checking over his shoulder to see if he could spot cameras or security guards. I reached my hand out and ran my fingers lightly over the frame. Nothing happened.

"Take it," he told me again.

And so I did. I pulled at the golden frame, surprised by how easily its weight shifted into my hand. Then I heard a horrible wail from an alarm. It whined and screeched until I let go and jerked my hand back. The painting wobbled and leaned sideways, so that the girl in the portrait was smirking at the ground. Two men in uniform appeared right behind me a moment later. "Astrid, what are you doing?" my grandfather asked in a shocked tone. "Don't touch that!" I turned to look at him, and he winked at me. He then spoke quietly to the two guards and flashed his congressional ID. He did that a lot when we went on trips. With that ID, he actually had diplomatic immunity, which meant that he could technically commit any crime he wanted to in another country and they couldn't do anything about it. I don't know how often he actually exercised this power, but I once saw him steal a Pez dispenser from a store in Berlin. The guards nodded to him, and we walked out of the museum.

"If you were quicker," he said, "you would have that damn painting. Astrid, never let anyone stop you from having everything you want."

"It's impossible, you know. I never could've had it."

"Impossible for everyone else, sure," he said. "Not for you and me."

>>>>>>>>>>>>>

I woke up in the nurse's office. I wasn't alone. That boy from class—the one with the weird shirt—was there. And he was staring at me.

"How long was I out?" I asked.

"You weren't really out. You were sort of muttering."

"What did I say?"

"Ms. Sharp asked if she should call an ambulance and you said, 'Not sure, I left my medical degree in my other purse. Why don't you figure it out yourself?'"

"Sounds like me," I said.

The nurse came from around a corner and handed me an ice pack. "Put this on your head," she told me. And then she looked at the boy and offered him a Popsicle. I had a pretty good feeling that an ice pack and a Popsicle were her go-to treatment options for everything. If you have non-Hodgkin's lymphoma and you seek treatment from the school nurse, you're going to get an ice pack or a Popsicle.

"You probably shouldn't sit up," he said.

"Are things blurry to you?"

"No. It's just you."

"Yeah," I said, "the world probably hasn't fallen out of focus for everyone since I've been out of it. How long have I been here?"

"Two periods, I think."

"That's a solid plus."

"I'm Noah," he told me.

"A pleasure, I'm sure," I said. "I'm Astrid Krieger."

"I know. I've heard about you. You're the girl who gets in trouble all the time."

"Thanks for the information, Einstein."

Noah blinked a few times, then leaned forward, propping his head on his palm. "Did you say that sarcastically because I said something you obviously already knew . . . or because you knew my name is Einstein?"

I looked at him, a little bewildered. "I didn't know you were named Einstein. I was being sarcastic."

"Good."

"Your name is really Einstein?"

He nodded. "Noah Einstein. Do you faint often, Astrid Krieger?"

"First time. Did I hit anything on the way down?"

"My desk," he said.

"Yikes," I said. "I didn't feel a thing."

"If you're okay, it's okay. It sure beats doing anything else. We missed math and gym entirely."

"If we can make this a regular part of our day, we could miss morning classes for the whole year," I said.

"That might lead to a permanent concussion."

"Suit yourself," I said, taking the Popsicle meant for him off the table. I ate it until my tongue was really purple. I stuck it out to make sure. There was something about me sticking out my tongue at him that made Noah's face fall. I had no idea why. Maybe someone he knew had a weird tongue disease, and he tried to think about it as seldom as possible. My thoughts were interrupted by a long, sustained beeping sound, which signaled the end of the period. According to my schedule, it was now time for lunch. "Do you know how to get to lunch?"

"Kind of," he said. "It's my fourth day."

"Did you eat lunch all of your first three days?"

"Nearly."

"Then you're not giving yourself enough credit," I said.

"Are you going to fall over again?" he asked as I began to stand up.

"I'll give you warning."

I always considered myself pretty skilled in figuring out what someone might be good at even if no one else could see it. I thought about a situation when I might need to execute some sort of elaborate plan and how I could use a guy like Noah. I couldn't think of one, but I figured he was worth having around anyway. Noah never found the cafeteria. After several tries, I had to ask a passerby. As far as Noah was concerned, from that point going forward he and I were friends.

# CHAPTER 6

# HOW I BECAME A FAMOUS BASKETBALL PLAYER

I love lunch. Particularly in school, but also just in general. I mean, what is there not to absolutely love about lunch? It's this break in the middle of the day where you get to eat and think about stuff and no one is pretending to teach you anything. When I was at Bristol, I would have my lunch in the dining hall. We were served by the work-study kids, and the food was usually pretty excellent. We could also go to a restaurant instead if we wanted, but there were only like two restaurants in the whole town and everyone would go to this diner that was supposed to look like the 1950s and people who worked there had to call you "Daddy-o" or "Betty." No thanks. When I didn't go to the dining hall, I went to my room and I could be free of everyone for an hour. So it was especially bad that lunch at Cadorette was as terrible as the rest of the day. You weren't allowed to leave. You had to be in the cafeteria, and the cafeteria was just full of the worst parts of the school—the worst parts of being seventeen in general—all jammed into one giant awful room.

I probably don't need to tell you what it's like in a public school cafeteria. I mean, it's very likely that you've been to one (or are sitting in one right now). And if you've seen one, I'm sure you've seen them all. But I'll describe it anyway in case you are homeschooled (in which case, your mom is probably really upset that you're reading this book because of the cursing. SHIT! SHIT! FUCK! SHIT!).

There were tables everywhere, and at every table sat an assortment of people who looked more or less like one another but unlike every other group in the cafeteria. Lucy was very excited when she described this breakdown to me and Noah. "You know, everyone sits with their friends." She didn't think much about the implications of her own seat at a fairly empty table way in the back corner. I was sitting there too, and I had a good idea of what it said about me. As far as Lucy was concerned, everyone was her friend, even the people who didn't look at her or listen to her. "I'm sure it was like that in your old school. I'm sure there were even more kinds of people."

"Just two kinds," I said. "Rich assholes and foreign people."

Lucy laughed, assuming I was joking. "But what about you?"

"Well, I don't speak Chinese, so . . . "

"It must've been terrible, then. All sorts of . . . *not nice people.*"

"I don't need nice people. I just need useful people."

"I don't understand," she said.

"It's what I'm good at. Everyone has a use. They don't always know what it is. I can usually figure it out." It was weird saying this to someone like Lucy, who pretty much had no use other than knowing the map of the school by heart. But she kept smiling the whole time I was talking, like she wasn't really listening anyway.

"Does being a friend count? As a useful thing?"

"No, Lucy," I said. "Being a friend does not count." I was suddenly pretty hungry. I looked around for the waiter.

Noah stood. "We have to go up," he said.

A few tables in front of us were filled with a bunch of boys wearing black T-shirts of seventies heavy-metal bands. They were probably having the same boring conversation about Led Zeppelin and guitars that boys had been having at that table for forty years.

In front of them were theater girls and boys. Some of them had on top hats. One of the girls had an actual monocle.

In front of them were the football players, all intently interested in a group of dull-looking girls. At the head of the table was the lazy-eyed girl in the stomach shirt from my English class. Those at the table—and frankly, it seemed like those everywhere—were waiting to hear whatever it was she was going to say next. They were almost panting. It was something resembling worship. It made absolutely no sense to me because I'm pretty sure the only areas in which she had any expertise were upper lip bleach and birth control.

Noah, Lucy, and I had to walk past her to get to the food. As we passed, she whispered something that made the whole table laugh. Not like the kind of laugh you might make when something is funny, either. It was the kind of laugh you make when you want someone to hear you laughing. I turned my head. It was just an instinctive move. People were being entertained by something, and I wanted to know what that something was. I turned to see what was so hilarious. But then I realized that they were laughing at me. It was the third time it had happened that day. First with the "princess" guy outside the school. Then with the "Ass-trid" boy in my English class. And now they were just laughing for no apparent reason. Just because they sort of knew who I was. This wasn't how I was used to being treated. I was used to being disliked, sure—even hated. I was used to being feared. I was not familiar with what it felt like to be openly mocked.

"It's okay," Noah said to me. "Ignore them. Let's get food."

I didn't understand girls at Cadorette. Up until now, my life had been filled with girls who were called Tibby and Bitsie (there are a hundred different nicknames for Elisabeth in my world). Girls with large vocabularies. Girls who spoke multiple languages. Girls who lost their virginity to Greek shipping magnates.

My very first day at Bristol, in chapel, Liddy Pierce came up next to me uninvited and, with some misguided sense that because our families owned neighboring villas in Italy, thought we were the sort of pair that would become friends. She sat down, looked around at half the student body, and sneered, "You know, there was a time when Bristol didn't even allow Jews."

I didn't look up from my fingers. "You know," I said, "there was a time when your parents and a surgeon had to decide whether the operation would make you a full boy or a full girl."

I glanced up in time to see Liddy's face turn completely white. After that, she walked away and never said a word to me ever again. "I know a guy who could shave down that Adam's apple," I yelled after her.

A really good insult only works if it's true. Thankfully, that one was. I'd spent the day before school boning up on administrative records. Survival isn't a race; it's a dance. It takes a certain grace and it also takes a lot of work. It's always best to be prepared.

But I was unprepared to deal with a girl whose parents had regular jobs and cooked dinner and shopped at outlet malls. She might have a switchblade in her teeth. I met girls like that in jail. But then again, girls had liked me in jail (they really had). These girls didn't like me. I had no idea what to do with them.

So I walked away. Noah, who had just met me that morning and only knew me as a girl who got in trouble a lot and fell on people's desks, was a little relieved I was avoiding confrontation. "People like that—they laugh at everyone," he said. This didn't make me feel better. I wasn't everyone.

"That's Summer Wonder," Lucy said, referring to the lazy-eyed girl. "We've been friends since second grade."

"Her name is Summer Wonder? Those were actual words that her parents thought sounded okay together?"

Lucy got nervous. "She can hear us." Lucy talked about her with a reverence that necessitated every detail be whispered. "Her father is Marvin Wonder," Lucy whispered. Then she nodded as if that was a satisfying biography.

"I have no idea what a Marvin Wonder is," I told her.

Lucy scrunched up her face in a sort of frustration and

pointed out the window across Mastracchio Road where a billboard showed a cartoon of a heavy, smiling, bald man making an introductory gesture toward a Ford truck. In bubble letters, the billboard read *Marvin Wonder Ford: The Lowest in Town.*

"The lowest what in town?" I asked.

"I don't know."

"Lucy," I said, with whatever sliver of confidence I had after Cadorette Township High School had chipped pieces of it away all day, "I'm Astrid Krieger. Do you know who my father is?"

I walked back over to Summer Wonder's table. "I don't want to do this," I said. "But there's something I need to tell you." I paused for what felt like forever. Her table quieted, anxious to hear what I would say. No one said anything for, like, a minute. "Oh man," I said, "I was really expecting something perfect to pop into my head but, Jesus, nothing's coming. Nevertheless . . . " There was a Twinkie lying on one of her friend's cafeteria trays. I picked it up and smushed it between my palms until my hands were covered in cakey goo. Then I wiped the doughy mess onto Summer Wonder's head.

I shrugged as if to say "not my best work," but it stopped her from laughing for sure. It also made it look like a bird had pooped in her hair. Everyone looked paralyzed by shock and confusion. No one knew what to do or what to make of me, so I didn't face any resistance as I walked away. I just really didn't want to be at that school anymore.

The rest of the week was just about as bad as I had imagined. And I have one hell of an imagination. I wasn't lucky enough to fall on someone's desk again, so I had to go to all my classes. English, math, and gym were in the morning. *Oh my god. Gym!* I had really thought I'd at least manage to get out of gym class. I mean, I'm good at getting out of stuff like that. It's kind of what I do. But somehow I lost that ability. I'd been failing at everything since I got kicked out of Bristol.

There were about five gym teachers. I focused on the oldest, manliest one and said, "I can't do gym, sir."

"Why is that, young lady?"

I didn't have a creative answer, but I had one that usually made men uncomfortable: "My period. I'm having my period."

But he didn't get uncomfortable. He just responded with, "Me too, dear." The oldest and manliest gym teacher was a lady. And then she insisted that I sign up for the basketball unit.

"But I don't like basketball. Honestly, I don't know anything about it. We didn't have the same sports at my last school. I assume you don't offer equestrian dressage in this gymnasium. Is there something in gym that involves sitting?"

"That's the reason you have to play basketball. It might surprise you. I think you might be a great basketball player."

That moment changed everything. The rest of this book is about how I became an incredible basketball player. I was a hero to the whole school. I won the big championship. I then became a professional basketball player and basketballed all over the world. But you already know that because I'm so famous for my basketball skills.

THE END

Okay. This is not a book about how I realized I was a great basketball player. Though I did realize something else: that if I just stood there, no one could really force me to do anything with the basketball. This was my goal for Cadorette in general: if I just stood there, people couldn't really give me any problems. At Bristol, I'd been different. I was always moving. I always had a plan and a reason. It was never to do homework or study or to maintain good grades but to intimidate everyone I disliked. I was trying to win at life. My family was already rich and powerful, and I'd been given a massive head start. But instead of winning, I'd just ended up at Cadorette. I didn't know how to win anymore. This place worked in entirely different currency. My wallet was stuffed with Confederate money. In a way, I'd already lost.

# CHAPTER 7

# THE ANEMONE

**L**ucy lived in a row of houses that all looked alike. They were beige and brick, and the only identifiable feature of hers was the cluster of balloons tied to the mailbox. Two balloons apparently meant "party time" in the Redlich house. The party started at six, which is ridiculously early, but I got there around eight. That was fine because the invitation told me it ended at ?, which meant that time was open to interpretation. It could last years.

I had my driver turn the car off, and I sat and thought for a minute about why exactly I'd come to Hair Eater's birthday party. I was not a fan of the idea of birthdays. There's no reason to celebrate the aging process. Birthday parties were like having breathing soirees or heart-pumping galas. They were celebrations of the mere act of existing. And I found that stupid.

After several minutes of me sitting, a very small car about the size of my outstretched arms pulled in front of the house. A little door opened. Noah stepped out and looked around.

"Drive!" I said to the driver. "Take me home." But then I quickly said, "Stop!" Noah was looking straight at the car, so my cover was blown. In the future if I wanted to be stealth, I probably wouldn't have a three-hundred-thousand-dollar, chauffeured Rolls-Royce slam on its brakes in the middle of a suburban housing development.

I got out and walked over to Noah. I tried to play it casual by making a joke about his tiny car. "When men have really ridiculous flashy cars, it usually means that they have small penises. Your car, I guess, points to a very big penis."

"It's my mom's car," he said. "She lets me borrow it."

"Your mom's penis must be enormous," I said.

"I didn't expect to see you here."

"I didn't expect to see me here either. But that's who I am—a master of what's not expected. Do you really want to go to this thing?"

"Of course. I'm here, aren't I?"

"Well, then so am I. Shall we?"

It was a long time before anyone answered the door. It felt even longer than that because I'm not good at small talk. Noah kept looking at me like I was supposed to ask him if he'd had a nice weekend or something. I wondered if maybe no one would ever open the door, and then I wouldn't get credit for going to the birthday party.

"Yes?" asked the woman who answered the door. She wore a nervous smile, as though afraid we were there to rob her.

"I'm Noah," Noah said. "This is Astrid. We're here for the birthday party."

Then the woman looked absolutely terrified. I wanted to assure her that we needed nothing from her, but then my mind wandered and I almost decided that we should try to rob her just to see what that would be like. She was an easy mark and would be too scared to tell the cops.

"I don't . . . I don't think there is a party anymore." She looked back into the house.

"No, there is," I said. "I got an invitation and everything. It was pink. There was glitter on it."

There was another long bout of silence, and then I heard Lucy from inside the house. "It's okay," she said. "They can come in."

The living room was small but bright. There were snacks on coffee tables and more balloons. But there was no music and no people. The place was untouched, as though it were a museum about birthday parties. Lucy was trying to bury herself into the side of the couch. She was chomping away at her hair in what was not a celebratory hair eating. It was the hair eating of sadness.

Noah walked in slowly and I followed because it had become pretty much impossible, by that point, to sneak away. He sat down on the couch next to Lucy and ate a corn chip with a hefty portion of lumpy, green-and-white mush. He smiled at her as if nothing was odd at all about the party. Then he asked a bit too enthusiastically, "What is in this dip? It's fantastic."

Lucy's mother gave a tight smile. "It's artichoke. And there's also crispy onions in it."

"Well," Noah said. "It's out of this world. Really. Good. Astrid, can I dip you a chip? You won't believe how good this is."

I sat down on the other side of the couch. "No," I said, "I believe you."

Lucy scooted over on the couch so she was now closer to Noah and me but still wrapped up in a tight ball. "No one . . ." she said really quiet.

"What?" I said.

"No one . . . came." This was pretty obvious at this point, though I hadn't said it out loud because there was no need. Lucy lifted her head so that she was looking right at me.

"I wouldn't say *no one* came," I said. "We're here."

"Thank you for coming," she said. "But I don't even want to think about what you must think of me."

Yes. She didn't want to know what I thought about her. But to be fair, no one has ever wanted to know what I thought about them. Almost everyone mentioned in this book probably should not be reading this book. But with Lucy—and in that moment—I didn't think of her any differently than I had before the guestless party. Why would I? "If I had a birthday party, no one would come either. Maybe Pierre, but that's a good reason to never have a party in the first place," I said. I wasn't trying to make her feel better. It was simply a fact.

"Ha, ha," Lucy said. "*Everyone* would come. I mean ... " Lucy trailed off and her lip quivered, which, coupled with her lisp, made her sound less like a person and more like an owl.

Noah stood up and sorted through Lucy's iPhone. "It's not a party without music, right?" he said, trying to change the subject. "We should dance or something . . . Is this whole playlist just French horn? Well, that's fine." And then Lucy and I were sitting on the couch while Noah tried his best to dance with no one to "Fanfare for the Common Man" while he insisted, "Come on, it's a party!" He was trying. And I could tell from his face that it wasn't easy. It was a depressing party. I'm sure there have been memorial services for school buses crashing into puppy stores with more celebration. There have been solitaire games with more people.

I stood up because by being there, I'd already completed the task I was supposed to. I didn't want to go to Lucy's birthday party (and here I hadn't thought I had anything in common with the rest of the school!), and my showing up was pretty much all Dean Rein had asked of me. He didn't expect me to change the world. I wasn't a magician. Also, where was the magician? I was pretty sure there was supposed to be one.

As I inched my way closer to the door, Noah changed his dance moves in a spastic maneuver that brought him very close to my face. "Where are you going?" he hissed at me through clenched teeth.

"There's no party," I said. "This isn't a party. I'm doing everyone a favor and putting this event out of its misery. Time of death: now."

Noah raised his eyebrow as if to say, *So that's who you are, huh?* And while it wasn't part of some elaborate plan to change my mind, it made me feel a pang in my gut. Meanwhile, Lucy and her mom both looked very helpless, and Lucy was tearing up. They didn't say anything, but it was as though they were asking me for something. They wanted me to do something. And I am the kind of person who does things. They're not always the right things or the good things, but I do things. My motto: Astrid Krieger: I Do Things.

I looked around the room for something I could use. Some good gear for epic revenge. There were chips. Balloons. Cake. A family portrait. A collection of porcelain elephants. An aquarium. A television. A bin full of umbrellas.

"Who was supposed to be here? Do you have a list?"

Lucy's mom nodded.

"The aquarium. Do you love each and every living thing inside?"

"They're my fish," Lucy said. "Of course I love them."

"Yes, but can we make a small sacrifice? In war, we sometimes must sacrifice those we love."

"We're not fighting a war," Noah said.

"My grandfather taught me that every day you're still alive, you'd better be fighting a war."

"Delightful," Noah said.

"He wouldn't like you either."

"What are you going to do with my fish?" Lucy asked.

"I don't need to use all of them. That's an anemone, right? The one that looks like . . . genitals?"

"It's not a fish," Lucy said.

"My grandfather used to do this thing in the navy. You

put one of them in someone's footlocker—or in this case, their house or car or sweatshirt . . . or school locker. The anemone is, like, ninety-nine something percent water and the rest is just shit. You anemone your enemy. The water evaporates and you're left with a smell that never goes away."

"Excuse me?" Lucy's mother said. I had turned her off completely.

"You want to do that to everyone who didn't show? There's only one anemone." Noah had a point.

"We can cover however many we can cover. Did Summer Wonder RSVP?"

"Yes," Lucy's mother said, a little unsure.

"A lot of people did," Lucy said. RSVPing to her party was probably a hilarious way for those people to prank Lucy. But pranks aren't funny when you target the weak. That's certainly not my style. What did Lucy ever do to anybody? Stupid people don't understand pranks.

"I'd love to hide this in her car. It'll make all of us feel better."

"I don't want to do anything mean," Lucy said.

"It's not mean. It's what's right."

"Maybe we should all go to the movies," Lucy's mother suggested.

"What do you want to do, Lucy?" Noah asked.

Lucy was quiet for a few moments. "Whatever Astrid wants to do for revenge sounds fun, sure. But I love my aquarium. I don't know. I'd also maybe go to the movies. Something romantic. Or a fantasy. But also something funny. A musical?"

Whatever fog of horrible sadness I had walked into was now—at least temporarily—lifted. In its place was a new problem—and that problem was me. I shouldn't have shown up. And I didn't want to spend the next two hours watching a funny romantic fantasy musical movie. I wanted to be alone. I went into my purse and left a hundred-dollar bill on the coffee table.

"You all should go to the movies together. Enjoy it."

"You're leaving?" Noah was incredulous.

"Yes, I think I am," I said.

Noah walked me to the corner and whispered, "You can't just throw money at her."

"Of course I can. And I did," I whispered back.

"She's sad. You can see that, right?"

"Of course she's sad."

"Look at her."

"What?" I said.

"Just look at her," Noah said.

And so I did. Lucy's eyes were downcast, and she was still biting on her lower lip. She gazed up at me with her pathetic face. She said, "Why do you think no one else came?" She was kind of asking everyone, but she was looking at me. No one wants to ever know the truth. Not about bad things. And I didn't know the true answer anyway, at least not for sure.

"I don't know," I said. It was the least horrible answer available to me.

She nodded anyway, as if I'd actually cleared up the matter. What I was feeling had to be what empathy was like. Dean Rein would be so happy to see me experiencing empathy. And suddenly, I couldn't leave. "Hey. Everyone," I said. (Only three people counted as everyone.) "Let's take this party on the road. I have a big car and a driver."

Lucy eventually chose to go to a roller-skating rink because I'd presented her with the option of going basically anywhere in the entire world, and she chose the worst option.

I had never roller skated before. I'm not good with things on wheels. I rented skates and moved out to the floor and *oh my god*, I was roller skating. I couldn't believe it. Within a second, I fell. Hard. Noah grabbed my hand to pull me up, but he's not very coordinated either, and so he fell. The next several minutes until I gave up were a constant exercise in standing and falling. Roller skating is fucking terrible. I can't express that enough.

I gave up quickly and crawled to the side of the floor. I sat there as people blew past me, sometimes backward.

Lucy whizzed by me. She could move fast. Her face was pink with a certain kind of happiness, and it was nice to see. She was happy, and I had helped with that. I'm not saying I changed the world or anything—I totally didn't, but I started to get why Dean Rein wanted me to do things I didn't want to do.

"Happy birthday," I called after her as she sped past me in her next lap. She waved, and when she did, her hair blew back, falling however briefly out of her mouth.

# CHAPTER 8

# THE GIRL WHO SET ME UP, OR "ONE EYEBROW"

**I**'d been thinking about Talia Pasteur a lot.

The night before I got expelled from Bristol, there was a party. As Pierre described it, "It is by the lake. There are some senior guys who have a rowboat." I wasn't sure what he was trying to say with that information. Was the party on the rowboat? Was the rowboat ferrying in supplies? Or did the rowboat have nothing to do with the party and Pierre was simply excited to have heard of a rowboat earlier in the day? Pierre was an idiot. Nonetheless, everyone I knew was going except for, well, me.

"You should attend," he said. "Dean Rein's office will still be there tomorrow." You see, the next Monday, there was to be a test in Dean Rein's class. That night, according to the plan, was the night we were going to get the answers. It wasn't just for me. It was for everyone. I was accused of being the one big cheater at Bristol, but truthfully, everyone cheated at Bristol. It was the way things were done. I was just really good at it.

When everyone else was at the rowboat party, I was outside the administrative building on my own—or so I thought, until I heard a wavering voice say, "You're soooo lucky." I looked over toward a collection of trees to see Talia Pasteur fall over, her face hitting the dirt. It does bear repeating that even dressed up for the lake party, she continued to look so much like a tree that she was nearly invisible until she collapsed.

She lifted her head, probably expecting me to pull her up. But I was still by the door to the administrative building. "I probably have dirt all over my face now," she said.

"Yeah. That's what happens when your face falls in dirt."

Talia was feebly drunk. Drunk-Talia was like one of those inflatable people with swinging arms outside car dealerships.

"Why am I lucky?" I asked her. I still have no idea why I decided to engage her, but my concentration was shot.

"Because he wants to be with you all the time. All the time, Astrid." Surprisingly, I understood what she was talking about. Talia had a burning crush on Pierre. It was a secret only to people who never talked to her. The fact that I was having a conversation about Pierre proved how unlucky I really was, thus collapsing her entire premise.

Talia pulled herself off the ground and brushed dirt off part of her cheek. "I just wanted to kiss him on the face."

"That's a really disgusting image you just gave me."

"What should I do, Astrid?" She swung her arm out toward my shoulder, either to hug me or kill a mosquito. I stepped back and gave her the opportunity to do neither. "I just need someone to tell me what to do," she said.

People like Talia always needed other people to tell them what to do. It's why she had such consuming crushes and almost nothing to say.

I didn't care what she did. Her love life may have been the single least important issue in the world. But like I said, I sort of liked Talia. She was almost a friend. Also, I happened to have a use for her at that moment. The lock to the administrative building had proven difficult to pick, and my master key had gone missing the year before. "You should throw a rock at that window."

"Why?"

"Don't you ever get so mad you need to just break something? You're carrying the weight of the world on your shoulders, Talia. It would really help."

Talia scrunched up her face so her eyes looked like

tiny slits extending from her nostrils. She picked a rock up from the ground and flung it. It didn't hit anything. It just fell on the ground.

"Why don't you try again, Talia?"

She pulled her arm back again, and this time, the rock hit glass, making a nice shattering sound. I nodded approvingly. Talia was out of breath like she had just had the most important experience of her entire life. "What do we do now?" she asked.

"Now?" I said. "Now we go inside."

>>>>>>>>>>>>

When I saw the all-new, blond Talia Pasteur with her stupid-looking mime makeup the week before, I felt a combination of shock and confusion. It was like trying to do a really hard math problem while also trying to swing on a trapeze. I may be overselling my feelings, but it was overwhelming given that I arrived at a bunch of very different conclusions all at once. Talia Pasteur had been planning her haircut and her eye makeup for months, maybe even years. Talia was ready to blossom— like when a tree becomes a butterfly. For whatever reason, Talia waited until I was out of the picture to make this big life change. That wasn't a coincidence. I decided that Talia Pasteur had wanted me out of Bristol. She was the person who set me up.

I had other suspects, sure. Others had wanted me gone. My grandfather has a phrase for people like us: "Heavy hangs the head that wears the crown." You may have heard that before. He didn't make it up (though he claims he did). What it means is if you are, say, Astrid Krieger, and life as Astrid Krieger is thoroughly and completely awesome, you should still watch out. It can be a pain in the neck (you know, because of that heavy crown). It's not all lollipops and rocket ships. People very often don't like me. (I know. Shocking.) Luckily for me, though, the people who haven't liked me have rarely been smart or clever.

I first suspected Whitney Brown of setting me up. My first year at Bristol, Whitney was running for freshman class student representative. She had a prominent unibrow and fingers like a lizard. I had known her since I was two, when we would quietly play with blocks and think about how much we hated each other. I remember her calling my stuffed bear "learning disabled."

Student government elections are a lot different at Bristol than they probably are at your school. At public school, someone's mom does her posters with Magic Marker. At Bristol, it's this whole thing with professional printers and attack ads. So Whitney Brown's father was actually running for Senate against my grandfather that same year and his stupid slogan was One Choice, One Connecticut, Carl Preston Brown. He lost. But not before Whitney ran for class president. So Whitney used the same printer and the same design, and her posters were supposed to say One Choice, One Year, Whitney Brown. I spent a late night wandering through campus and blacking out certain letters on her posters (specifically, *Choice On ar Whitney* and *n*) so her campaign slogan became One Eye Brow. She had like a thousand of those posters printed, and she was super angry. (She shouldn't have been because she actually won. People loved voting for "One Eyebrow." And I didn't care either way.) Do you want to know how she tried to get me back? By hanging a bucket of water over my door. Seriously. If her plan had been executed perfectly, I would have opened my door and the bucket of water would have fallen on my head. And then what? I'd have gotten a little wet. Who cares? I could just dry myself and change clothes in my room, which is where the bucket-holding door was. Straight-up amateur hour. I decided that there was no way Whitney set me up. She never could have been so innovative.

What was just so unbelievable about Talia Pasteur is that she tried to get me kicked out of Bristol and succeeded. I honestly didn't think she had it in her. I would have admired her if I wasn't so mad at her. I never thought much of Talia at Bristol. I certainly didn't hate her. We weren't friends, but she was the closest thing to a friend I had. When I was stealing term papers or buying fireworks, she was usually there. Talia wasn't my enemy. I didn't understand why I was her enemy. We weren't equals. I was the shark and she was the little fish sharks barely even notice. Why would she have wanted me out of school? I could have thought of a hundred reasons a hundred people other than Talia Pasteur would have wanted me out of Bristol, but none of the people with those reasons had done it. The good news is, I could beat girls like Talia while blindfolded and drowning in a pool filled with vanilla ice cream, caramel syrup, and maraschino cherries. What were we talking about? I could super use a sundae.

I was going through all of these thoughts aloud during an art class at Cadorette. (They called it an art class, but they didn't have the money to actually make us do anything. So it was more of an exercise to see what people nearly old enough to vote could do with construction paper, paste, and finger paints.) And when I say I was saying my thoughts aloud, I mean that Pierre was there, but when I talk to him, it's basically like monologuing. This time around, he seemed too busy trying to form a paper clip into a dog to even listen. But after I'd finished addressing most of my Talia-related stuff, he looked up as though he'd been paying attention all along. "She wrote to me," he said.

"Who wrote to you? Talia?"

"Yes."

"Did she say anything about me?"

"She didn't *not* say anything about you. It was between the lines. She was disappointed that I left Bristol. She says it is like a whole new school now. That I would like it there."

"And?"

"She wants to talk to me."

"About me?"

"She didn't actually mention you." He very slightly touched the edge of my pinky finger with his pinky finger, causing me to jerk my hand back. "But if she is anything like me, she was thinking about you with every word."

"You're incredibly helpful, Pierre."

"Thank you, my dear."

"I didn't actually mean that. I meant the opposite of that."

"Ah, yes, that is sarcasm you are so fond of." I was sure they had sarcasm in Pierre's language, but he always treated it like some magical new invention.

"I am glad I go to this school, now," Pierre said. "Don't you?"

"No, Pierre. No, I don't."

"Really? It's wonderful here." Pierre had immediately thrived at Cadorette. Girls found him funny and exotic and guys found him impressive. They made him the kicker for the football team. "It is a very funny story," he said. "The boys, they asked me if I play football and then they qualified and said that they know that what I call football is what they call soccer. And I told them that what I call football is what they call football and what they call soccer is actually what I call *fotbalový*."

"That might be the least funny story I have ever heard in my entire life," I said. "I have heard funnier stories about the Bataan Death March."

Pierre went on as if I had just agreed with him. "So they asked me if I could kick and they said that their kicker fell to injury. They looked at me and must have seen my masculine energy and knew I was needed on their team."

"It's a very masculine position, Pierre. Do they provide you with the ballet slippers or do you bring your own?"

"I bring my own," he said. "You will cheer me on for the big homecoming game, I hope."

Homecoming had quickly become the most important topic in the lives of the poor, poor morons at Cadorette and I had a hard time figuring out what I was supposed to think about it because I was sad to admit that I was one of those poor, poor morons. Pierre was very excited about it.

"Do you think they'll have hip-hop music and streamers and do you think they will play 'In Your Eyes'?" he asked. Pierre got incredibly excited when anything in his life remotely resembled a movie about a fifteen-year-old girl struggling with love and her burgeoning desires. "Don't make any big plans," he said. "I am going to ask you to the homecoming dance in a big way but I have yet to sort out the details."

"I think I'm committing seppuku that evening."

"You are what?"

"It's Japanese ritual disembowelment with a sword. It's how I would prefer to spend that night."

"You are very hilarious, Astrid," Pierre said.

Pierre drove me to Bristol for my next appointment with Dean Rein. It was a horrible ride. He had a car, but we took his motorized scooter instead. It wasn't comfortable for two people, and it hit a breezy thirty-five miles per hour on the highway. I thought we would die a hundred times. Ordinary death paled in comparison to dying while clutching Pierre's waist. My obituary would exist forever, calling him my boyfriend and mentioning that I died after being thrown from a lavender Vespa. I decided that I should really learn to drive very, very soon. I would never again have to hear Pierre's music mixes, and I would never again have to hear him say through the buzzing of his Vespa's little engine: "The words of this song translate to 'My love is strong like the crust of mountains and soft like bales of cotton.' Love is confusing. It is both things."

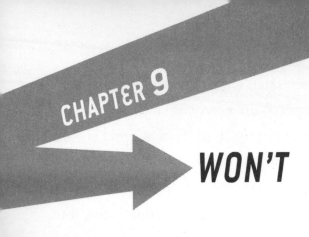

# CHAPTER 9

# WON'T

I was twelve, and it was Christmas afternoon. Vivi and my dad were away in Abu Dhabi in a palace. It belonged to a college friend of Dad's who called himself Marc, although his name was not really Marc. He had a scar that stretched clean across his face and a fake finger made out of ivory. (The richer you are, the more likely you'll have friends with body parts made out of elephants. It's weird but true.) Lisbet had received a kite that morning and was off somewhere trying to figure out how to make it work. (She never did.) And so it was just me and my grandfather in the house. Neither of us was what I would call "Christmas people." We hated lights, trees, singing, snow, movies with lessons, and shopping malls. Pretty much the only worthy part of Christmas we could both agree on was presents, and we didn't need a special day to get stuff.

We had our own traditions, and they were the high point of every December. The staff would be off, so we'd make lunch out of whatever we could find. That year, it was a sandwich of marshmallows, salami, honey cashews, grapes, lemon meringue pie, and brie. (I know that sounds disgusting and . . . well, it was.) Then we would read Lisbet's diary. Then prank call the president of the United States (who could never take a joke). Then we would drive into the town square and shoot BBs at the municipal nativity scene. If any cops were around, my grandfather would mutter something like, "Do you know who I am?" and "diplomatic immunity," and people would leave us alone.

But my heart wasn't in it that year, and I wasn't even looking when he nailed a direct shot between the eyes of a wise man.

"Okay, enough of this," he said. "What the hell is with you, anyway?"

"Nothing," I said. But my voice was shaky.

"Is it gonna be a whole day of this?"

"I've been fine all day."

"Nuh-uh. You've been no fun. I haven't heard you laugh once."

"Maybe nothing's been funny."

"Lisbet's diary, when she called it her 'special monthly lady adventure'? Hilarious."

"I'm perfectly fine. I'm always fine, you know," I said.

"There are a million things I can do without you, if you

don't want to be here," he said. "I enjoy you, Puppy, but without you around, I can get drunk in a hotel bar." He jangled his car keys as if it were a threat. "What the hell is wrong with you?"

I avoided his eyes. "I can't tell you," I said, "because it's the sort of thing you told me you never wanted me to tell you about."

He made a grunting noise. "It's a boy, huh?" He looked down at his shoes. "I didn't say 'never tell me about it,' I just said I wouldn't like it. Just tell me. You can tell me. But avoid the mushy stuff because I just ate a pound of butter."

"It's not mushy," I said. "I promise you that. I promise you that it will never be mushy. I'm mostly disgusted at myself."

The week before, a boy had asked me if he could be my boyfriend. I thought I liked him. His name was Will, but he called himself "Won't," and that's exactly the sort of thing a twelve-year-old might find interesting. (I was dumber when I was twelve than I am now.) I now know that "Won't" is about the stupidest nickname in the world. And also, every nickname is stupid if you pick it for yourself. You should never get to pick your own nickname.

At the time, I was attending an all-girls school in Massachusetts called St. Anianus, where the name was the only entertaining thing about the place. And really, after three days spent saying "Stainy Anus" out loud, it was just another school. Won't went to Admiral Sanders down the street. It was a military school and possibly also a chicken restaurant. Military schools were for bad kids. For me, having that place full of delinquents so close was good because bad kids had things I needed. I met Won't because he sold me cherry bombs, firecrackers, and sparklers. I needed to set them off in a nun's toilet (this was a Catholic school). We ended up talking for a few hours about all sorts of romantic things like lock picking and how to make napalm. When I was about to leave, he asked if he could kiss me, and I really couldn't think of a good reason why not. No one had ever kissed me before, and Won't had his mysterious nickname. So, he stuck his spongy tongue in my mouth for twenty seconds. It was not without its charm. I said what I thought I was supposed to say, "I think I like you," and then he said, "Cool. You too." And I walked away with that goofy, smiley expression that girls I hate always have on their faces.

"You're overreacting. Hate to say it, but you'll probably kiss all sorts of slimy boys in your life. Nothing to cry about," my grandfather said.

"It's not that. The slimy kiss was fine. The problem was two days ago. I was coming home. I had the driver stop down the street so I could get coffee, and a lot of kids from school were there. And Antonia VeraCruz—"

"With the teeth?"

"She was there. And a bunch of other kids. And she just comes up to me and says, 'I never could figure out why you think you're so much better than the rest of us. But now I know,' she said. 'You're not.'"

"Hmm. Go on."

"And then I saw where she was sitting, and he was there. Won't was right next to her."

"It bears repeating: terrible nickname. Confusing in conversation."

"And they all said, 'I think I really like you,' in this stupid voice that I think was supposed to be my voice. I think maybe she put him up to being my boyfriend. It made me sad. Like *really* sad."

Grandpa took a flask from his jacket and took a sip. He offered me one, but I was fine (and, as I mentioned before, twelve years old). "First of all, you *are* better than they are. Kissing a greasy punk doesn't change that. That's for sure. Who are you mad at, her or him?"

"Everyone. The world. But more him. I let my guard down. I shouldn't have done that."

"Boys, they're worth nothing. Their hormones and their face acne. They're disgusting. I know because I was one, and that part of me—the disgusting part—still owns a hell of a lot of real estate in my brain."

"I feel stupid, you know. I feel like I let someone stupider than me outsmart me."

"Yeah. I'll say that's about right. What are you going to do about it?"

"I found a man with a gambling problem at the county records office. For a small fee, he'll change the date on Won't's birth certificate. Then I'm going to enlist him in the army."

"Not this time," he said quickly. "Let it go, Astrid."

"You want me to forgive him?"

"Forgiveness," he said, "is for those too weak to hold a grudge. But I want you to stop caring about him. You can give him a bad day, but he'll have a bad life without your involvement. He calls himself Won't, for chrissake. Just walk away knowing you learned a lesson. You're not going to trust someone so easily again, so that's good."

"It'll never happen again. Boy stuff. It's not me, so I'm done."

Grandpa squinted in a deep thought for almost a minute. "That's fine," he said. "You won't get pregnant. You won't have some little bastard with a Kool-Aid mustache running around the house, asking for money. The fewer boys around here, the better."

"So we agree."

"Nah. It won't work. You say it now, but it won't work. I promise you that."

"I'm not Lisbet, you know. I'm not the kind of girl who needs mushy stuff. I'm done. I'll sign a piece of paper affirming this fact."

"Here's the thing about being young," he said, "and I'm not saying 'here's the thing about being a kid' 'cause you're not a kid. You haven't been one since you were a baby and I wouldn't insult you by calling you a kid. Your sister's a kid. Your father's a kid. But you're no kid."

"Thank you," I said.

"But you're young. So, here's the thing about being young: as smart as you are, as much as you know who you are, as much as I respect you—and I'm telling you, I don't respect anyone else—just you, and maybe my bookie. But this is true of every young person because it was true for me. You believe a lot of things right now, but there are at least three very important things that you won't believe anymore when you get old. That happens to everyone, and you're not so special that it won't happen to you."

"You don't believe me, then?"

"It's not that I don't believe. You may hate boys every day for the rest of your life. So then there will be three other things that won't be true anymore. And you are just going to have to make your peace with it."

"What were those three things for you?"

"Not sure yet. I'm old, but I'm going to be older still."

>>>>>>>>>>>>>

Dean Rein held the piece of paper with my list of things between his thumb and his forefinger. He barely looked at it. "I thought you wanted to change, Astrid." Dean Rein was trying a different way of talking to me. He didn't smile in the usual, fake-friendly way.

"What makes you think that? When did I say that?"

"You didn't. But I sensed it. You're here, aren't you?"

"You sensed it because I'm here? I *have* to be here."

"You don't have to be anywhere. You always have a choice, Astrid."

"I do?" I asked. Then I stood up and left.

I was one step out his office door when he yelled after me. "If you leave, you're going to lose."

This stopped me. I looked back at him over my shoulder. "I wasn't aware that we were having a contest, sir."

"Well, we are always in the middle of a contest, Astrid. And you're about to lose. You don't like to lose, do you?"

In fact, I hate to lose. Always have. Always will. "I did what you asked. I did stuff I didn't want to."

"You went to a birthday party and tried to steal a fish. I'm having a hard time wrapping my head around how that met any of the requirements I laid out for you."

"A sea anemone isn't a fish."

"I stand corrected."

"We went roller skating. I hated every second of that."

"You kept the whole birthday party experience at a distance. You didn't let yourself be a part of it."

"You know, I could've just lied and said I spent the week building homes for the homeless, but I didn't because I thought I did a pretty good job. Also, there were a lot of times that I could've said something really mean and I didn't. I could've told Lucy, 'No one came because you eat your own hair and you talk weird,' but I didn't. I said nothing. That's an achievement for me."

"You're saying that you should get credit for something you didn't say but could've said. Astrid, not doing something is not the same as doing something."

"That's very inspiring. You sound like the Buddha. You should write fortune cookies."

"This doesn't count, Astrid."

"I made a friend, I think. The one I fainted on," I said. "That was a really big deal for me."

"You fell on his desk. If you had fallen a few inches in the other direction, you wouldn't have made a friend with anyone."

"You were never that specific in terms of what you were looking for me to do." The words were no longer on my hand, but as I understood them, *do things you don't want to do* pretty much meant exactly what it said. It was simple, but Dean Rein wanted to make it difficult. He wanted me to want to do the things I didn't want to do. I was getting a headache just trying to make sense of it.

"I can't be any clearer. You needed to do good things. Good deeds. And you didn't, so you lost. You went through the motions of one relatively good deed, sure. But I asked you for three. And if you try to change your behavior while continuing to keep the world at arm's length, you'll never make any strides. Remember, Astrid, you can't have your cake and eat it too."

"What do you mean?" I asked. "What reason would you want cake other than for eating?"

"It means—"

"Are you telling me there are people in this world who have to decide whether or not to eat a cake or just display it in their homes? Like, 'Please come over to my house and see my glass display cases of old moldy cakes'?"

"It means you can't have it all, Astrid."

"Of course you can. Why wouldn't you just buy two cakes? I mean, if you're the kind of person who is so into keeping cakes, just splurge. Live a little. Buy another cake. You only live once, Dean Rein."

"Are you done?"

"Let me just say this—as a friend—maybe you could stand to eat less cake, sir."

"I want you to do this little task again. But this time, please perform real selfless acts."

I looked out his window. The sky was blue. The grass was green. Someone was riding a horse through the trail on the quad. If Dean Rein was powerful, he probably would've orchestrated my view to look exactly like that. To show me how different Bristol was from the school I would have to go back to the next day. I had a thought. A thought that I figured would probably work. "Care to make it interesting?" I inquired.

"Oh, Astrid, this is my job. It'll never be interesting."

I ran my thumb over the tips of my fingers, the international symbol for *I have invisible money in between my fingers.*

"I'm not putting any money on this. I get paid to be here," he said. "Plus, you have a lot more money than I do, so what do you stand to gain?" This was of course true for him and almost everyone.

"Then how about I do the good deeds challenge? And if I do it well, I don't have to come here anymore."

"Again," he said, "I make money by you being here. Your parents are paying me. Money for my time is very agreeable to me."

"Then . . ." I looked out the window and I couldn't help but smile. "How about we bet on Bristol? If I win, I get to come back to school here."

"That's not entirely up to me."

I knew he would say something like that, but I didn't really buy his argument. "Yes it is. You are the dean of students and I am a prospective student, Dean."

"I'd have to convince your parents."

"I convinced my dad that the whole world travels back in time for daylight savings. Just say it in a serious voice. He'll believe anything."

"Fine," Dean Rein said. "Do real good things. Three of them. Write them down. Include proof where available. And if they're acceptable, that's certainly something we can discuss."

"Uh-uh, not discuss. If I do it, I come back to Bristol. They will be good deeds. Great deeds."

He didn't respond aloud, but his silence was enough for me. Ultimately I felt like I was going to get what I wanted. I wanted to go back to Bristol, and if he felt like he somehow set me on a path to be a better person and could smugly pat himself on the back, it was totally fine with me. Maybe I was already on my way to becoming a good person. I probably should've just quit right there.

# CHAPTER 10

# I RODE INTO THE SUNSET

**P**ierre couldn't manage to wait outside for the hour I was with Dean Rein. I should've figured that he would follow whatever weird impulse he had. In this case, he wanted to ride a horse to go talk to Talia Pasteur. Pierre talked to Talia regularly when he went to Bristol. Like many people, Pierre enjoyed conversations with people who would agree with pretty much everything and rarely interrupt. By the time I walked outside, Pierre had galloped halfway across campus. In place of him, there was a small freshman with a rather severe haircut standing at the bottom of the steps of the administration building.

"Are you Astrid Krieger?"

"Who are you?"

"Andy Chang." What is with people thinking that if you don't know who they are, their name is sufficient explanation? "The guy with the long hair told me to wait for you."

"Where is he?"

"He said he went to talk to the person that he needed to talk to."

"Where?"

"Her room."

"Where is her room?"

"How would I have any idea?" Andy Chang asked. He had a point. I turned, intending to wander around and figure it out. "Are you really Astrid Krieger?" Andy Chang called out behind me.

"Why wouldn't I be?"

"I've heard of you. But you are not what I thought you would be."

"What did you think I would be?"

"I thought at least you would be taller." This was the strangest and most upsetting thing anyone had said to me in the last month, even though it kind of didn't make any sense (because I, being Astrid Krieger, was exactly as tall as Astrid Krieger should be). But, I don't know. Maybe Astrid Krieger the person and Astrid Krieger the reputation were no longer the same thing. I was still Astrid Krieger, but the Legend of Astrid Krieger was slowly fading away. It was almost as if I had gone back in time and somehow made my dad's fiancée not die in that helicopter crash, thereby preventing him from meeting my mother at the hospital where she was working as a nurse, hence eliminating my existence. Astrid Krieger the legend was as tall as a mountain. Astrid Krieger the person wasn't much more than five feet two inches, except in heels.

>>>>>>>>>>>>>

Suddenly I knew where Talia Pasteur's room was. Talia Pasteur's room was my room. It would really be the only place that would make sense. I'd had the biggest room on campus. This was because it was a room meant for two people. My roommate, Yves Graneveis, was the daughter of a French diplomat. As far as the administration was aware, Yves's arrival in the United States had been held up for several years at that point due to an Interpol investigation into her family surrounding the kidnapping of her brother, Gaston. The administration at Bristol was very understanding throughout the ordeal and promised to keep her bed available to her if and when her circumstances changed and she was ready to begin her education at Bristol. Of course, I completely made Yves Graneveis up, but she has a very believable passport, a Canadian medical license, and owns a minority stake in a chain of fine men's clothing stores in the Midwest.

When I got to Ladies' Dorm 3 (they used all the good dorm names like "Hampshire Hall" and "Woodmeadow Residence" on the boys' dorms), I saw Pierre on a horse and Talia skipping over to him from the east side of campus. I hadn't been spotted yet, and I couldn't think of a particularly stealthy way to spy. I wished that I had a Gatling gun. I also wished I had the ability to climb walls. There were a lot of graceful and death-defying things I wished that I could do at that moment. But I didn't have any of the tools or magical abilities required, so instead I dove down and crawled under a bush. This was not ideal. I was getting mud on my hands and clothes. I was pretty sure I'd never hidden from anything. As a kid, I played hide-and-seek by sitting on a bench.

I had a pretty good view of the horse's tail. Horses smell bad from the front, but it's much worse when your nose is seven inches from one's anus. I could only hear pieces of their conversation through the sound of the horse stomping on leaves.

What I heard was this:

Talia: You showed up——surprised——let you—— does that.

Pierre: I am my own——-That is——understand.

Talia: I hope you know————when she—— Astrid————strid.

Pierre: Please, you have to know that I————What do you think—————? She isn't making it.

Talia: I'm sure she's doing fine—————what she deserves anyway—————found out about us.

Pierre: There is an us?————forever————is what I think. She doesn't know—————-about—————

Talia: She doesn't? I doubt that. Hello, Astrid———strid—————in the bush—————I see you. Yes. I see you.

The jig was up. I thought about staying in the bush forever, maybe building a life down there just to prove that I had some other reason for being there, but I knew that she knew my real reasons. I'd been stupid. If anyone could spot somebody else hiding in shrubbery, it was Talia. It's like how my mother can tell which actresses on TV have cheekbone implants.

I stood up—I was covered in filth. I stayed stoic, but I must have looked like a goddamn hobo.

"You brought her, then? You said you came alone," Talia said to Pierre.

He shrugged. "I will always be prepared to lie for her."

"You shouldn't have to," she said. Talia's look had changed even more in the previous week. She had on leather wristbands and hair extensions on only one side. She looked like she was tilting her head to the right, even though she wasn't. "He won't say it," Talia told me as she chewed on her thumbnail with venom. "So you say it. Why are you here?"

"I have my reasons."

"I know your reasons. You meet with Dean Rein every week because you're crazy." A small crowd had gathered. I noticed Andy Chang—the freshman with the bad hair—and Joe Flemming, who I used to employ for his computer expertise, in the back of the crowd. Maribelle Rohit, whom I'd utilized for her acting ability, was just behind Talia. If this was a war, they were definitely on her side of the battlefield. They were scared of her. I could tell because they used to be scared of me.

"I'm not crazy. There are a lot of not-crazy people in therapy." Ugh, looking back, I still can't believe I quoted my mother.

"You see everybody all around here, we all go to school here. *You don't*. Go home, Astrid."

"You know what you did, Talia." I just figured I would come right out and say it. Maybe it would work. Maybe I would break her under cross-examination.

"What did I do?"

"I trusted you, and you're the one who got me kicked out." I gave her a hard stare. The sort that makes people tremble. I saw a few of the sophomores shake a bit.

"You trusted me, Astrid? Really? Were we ever friends?"

"We were friends . . . ish."

"I thought we were friends once. But I was silly and naive. I'm not so naive anymore. You're a liar, a cheater, and a thief; and you got kicked out because you're a liar, a cheater, and a thief."

I let that roll around in my head a little bit. She had a point, but I couldn't let her know that. "You sent those tests to Dean Rein, though. You set me up."

"I didn't."

"You did."

"I didn't."

I was about to get stuck in one of those back-and-forth loops that could go on for weeks. Let's just say it went on, like, nine more times. Pierre was the one who broke it. "Astrid will prove it."

"I will!" I said. *I would?*

"So prove it," Talia said, calling Pierre's bluff. She had me. Again. I couldn't prove that she'd done anything. I felt it inside, but I didn't really know how I could prove anything. I could make something up, but that probably wouldn't work. Maybe if I pulled a magical map from my pocket and said, *I found THIS!* it would work. She wanted me to prove her guilt, and I needed to figure out how. Without evidence, there was nothing to say it really was she who set me up. That was what a lawyer would have told me, anyway. I wasn't a lawyer, but I know how to say "objection" and "overruled." Just then, I had to back down. But I needed to do it in a way that didn't make me seem like a total failure. I needed people to know that I was still Astrid Krieger. I was exactly as tall as I should be. Talia was an imitation, a fake, a blurry photocopy. Because I had no other options, I got on the horse and rode away. I didn't have to look back to know that everyone was watching me. I only hoped they didn't see me get off the horse on the other side of the parking lot and wait twenty minutes for Pierre to find me before abandoning the horse for his stupid scooter.

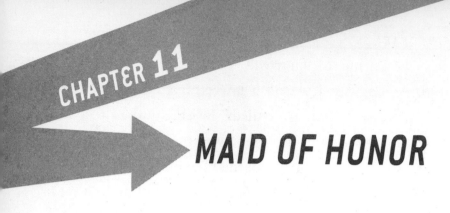

# CHAPTER 11

# MAID OF HONOR

I had accepted Dean Rein's challenge. I was about to do all sorts of incredibly good things. It was like putting on new clothes. I actually tried to say it to myself in the mirror:

"Astrid, you're a good person." Then I laughed. Trying to see my reflection as a good person was almost like seeing myself with a mustache.

I started to make a list of really good things I could do, but I didn't get very far. My mind wouldn't go there. I decided instead that I should maybe just ask a good person for advice and steal her answers. It wouldn't really be stealing so much as borrowing.

My house was not full of good people. My grandfather was the most like me, so it was safe to say he wasn't good. My mother was awful. My father wasn't bad, but he was too lazy to do much good. That left Lisbet. Was Lisbet a good person? Lisbet was certainly a nice person. But was that the same as good? Some people would say so. And being nice is a very important part of being good. How much a part of it, I wasn't positive, but I thought I might as well ask her before going to anyone else.

I found Lisbet in her bathroom, where she can usually be found in the mornings. A good chunk of her time there was spent dallying with makeup and hair-related issues. But, mostly she just sat there, happily smiling at her reflection. I was years past finding this weird.

While Lisbet's fiancé, Randy, lived in the guesthouse with Lisbet, he would leave early in the morning for work—sometimes while I was still awake from the night before. He worked either far away or long hours or both. When Lisbet first met him, she told me what he did for a living. He was a lawyer or banker or fireman or astronaut or horse whisperer or candy maker or something. He was not so successful that they lived somewhere else but not so unsuccessful that he didn't need to comb his hair and put on a tie and go to the office.

I knocked. Knocking was always a good idea. There were things you just didn't want to walk in on people doing. I learned that lesson when I was in boarding school in Switzerland. I had a roommate then. She had a name, of course, but I couldn't think of her as anything other than Girl Who Licks My Used Tissues When She Thinks I'm Not in the Room.

Lisbet didn't answer when I knocked, so I cracked the door and yelled her name a few times.

"I'm so glad you could come see me, Astrid," Lisbet said, staring deeply at her reflection while perched on a tufted stool in front of her vanity. Lisbet had this thing where if you and she were ever in the same place, she would assume that she asked you to be there. Once I was in the elevator at our dad's office and she happened to be there too, and she said, "I'm so glad you could make it, Astrid," as if she'd scheduled this elevator get-together. *11:08 on the east, middle elevator. We will meet for nineteen seconds until the door opens again.*

"I wanted to ask you something," I told her. I leaned back against the mural of a foxhunt that was painted above the wainscoting. After Lisbet moved into the guesthouse, she'd added smiles to most of the foxes with acrylic paint.

"And I wanted to ask *you* something." She addressed my reflection in her mirror.

"You first."

"No, you first," she said.

"Why are you nice, Lisbet?" I said.

"Why am I nice? I don't understand."

"You know how I have to do all this stuff now?"

"Stuff you have to do?" Lisbet absolutely never remembered backstory. If you were watching a movie with her, you'd need to re-explain who the cop was and who the murderer was multiple times. And when she called me on the phone, she would sometimes say, "It's your sister . . . Lisbet." As though I had more than one sister.

"I'm going to the school in town. I have to go to therapy. That stuff."

"Of course. Yes. How's that working out for you? I'm very worried about it."

"It's awful, Lisbet. I'm constantly miserable."

"And you want some tips from me about how not to be miserable?"

"No. It's more about . . . how you're a good person."

"Me?" She gave herself a hard and probing stare in the mirror, apparently considering it. "I don't think so. I'm normal. I'm not especially good."

"Well, you're probably the most good person I know." ("Most good person," by the way, is very different from the "best person" I know. I'm the best person I know.)

Lisbet laughed. Or at least, it sounded like it was supposed to be a laugh. It was more like a quiet hoot. "I couldn't be the best person you know. What about Ginny Ford?"

"Who's Ginny Ford?"

"I guess you don't know her. She's very considerate. I'm surprised the two of you haven't met."

"What I mean, Lisbet, is that people like you. You're nice to everyone. You seem to make an effort with people . . . I'm kind of wondering how you do it."

Lisbet didn't say anything for about a minute. "It's easy, Astrid." I waited for her to say something else, but she didn't. We both stared at Lisbet's face in the mirror.

"It's easy . . . what?"

"It's easier, I mean. It's easier for me to be nice than to not be nice. Do you remember Griffin Hammett?" Griffin Hammett was Lisbet's boyfriend for the majority of the time she was at Bristol. We only overlapped briefly at that school, so I only knew about him from the letters Lisbet wrote me. Lisbet and I had a one-sided correspondence. She liked to write letters and send them in the actual mail. She and my grandfather are probably the last people in the world who do things like that. She would write me letters about all sorts of stupid stuff like "I ate a salad" and "If you can remember, please answer my question from my last letter. I really need to know how to spell his name so I can tell my doctor." More and more the letters were about Griffin Hammett. And because she's Lisbet, the letter might say, "Have I told you about Griffin, my boyfriend of two years?" Griffin visited Lisbet at the estate the summer after my first year and her last year at Bristol. I was just passing through for a week before my parents sent me to Australia. Griffin was sleeping in the guest-house—the very same house I was standing in right then. My first impression of him at school and at the Krieger Estate was that he was relatively harmless, but he had an annoying way of telling you how he did something once just slightly better than you. If there was wine served with dinner, Griffin would say, "My parents love that bottle, though they normally drink the 1990." Or, "Spain is nice, but for an authentic Spanish experience you should really go to Portugal." Or, "Your pants have two legs in them. Well, my pants have three legs in them. Four, even." He was annoying, but who cared, right? I wasn't the one writing his last name next to my first name surrounded by a cloud of loopy hearts on every piece of paper in sight.

I could've easily left for Australia and lived my whole life never thinking of Griffin Hammett again unless he married Lisbet and they had children. But that didn't happen. Instead, I remember him because Griffin was a lot slimier than I'd originally thought. I was staying in my old bedroom, which was on the third floor. It was out of the way, the kind of place people would only end up in if they were really looking for me. I wasn't sleeping yet, but it was late at night. My door opened, and there was Griffin in these silk pajamas that my dad also wears. "What do we have here?" he said. "You waited up for me."

I didn't look up. I didn't give him the benefit of acknowledging he was even in the room. I just lifted my head a little bit and said, "I have a knife. I have several."

Griffin laughed and shook his head. "I have a lot I could teach you, you know. I'm really upset at your sister because she never once told me that you were so pretty."

I reached toward the side of my bed, which was exactly where my grandfather told me I should keep my knives. I was pretty sure I had one, but as it turned out, I didn't. I did have scissors, though. "I'm seriously not lying about my knife," I said.

He laughed again and sat down slowly on the edge of my bed. He wasn't right next to me, but he was within arm's reach. "Those are scissors," he said, noticing the scissors.

"Scissors are two knives with a screw in the middle."

"What'll you do if I keep sitting here? Stab me? Or make me some paper dolls?"

I shook my head. "No. I would never stab you."

"Good," he said, and reached his hand over to my bare leg. He then gripped it like I was a tennis racquet.

I reached my hand out to touch his hair. He smiled but looked not the least bit surprised. He was completely surprised a minute later, though, which was weird because I'd been pretty up front the whole time. I grabbed a clump of his hair with one hand and cut the hair off with the scissors. I then tossed his hair on top of his head, and it fell all over his face. There are still pieces of hair hiding everywhere in that room.

Griffin stammered and ran out of the room. I heard him crying and yelling, "She's crazy! She's nuts!" as he ran down the stairs. I'm not sure how he explained any of it to Lisbet, but to her infinite credit, she believed me. I don't even know if I would believe me in the same situation. She didn't break up with him, though. Not immediately. Being too nice is her curse, I guess. She had to wait until he left her for this girl Marjorie, who had known Lisbet since they were both six. After that, I paid Joe Flemming to alter a few details of Griffin's life on the Internet, and now whenever you search his name, you find out that he's a registered sex offender. He wasn't, but I figured it was just a matter of time.

"I could've never done what you did to him, with the hair and everything," Lisbet said in her bathroom.

"Why not? You have to stand up for yourself."

"Oh, that's all fine. I take kickboxing classes at the gym. That's not what I mean. I just would never have thought about it. It's too hard to think like you do."

"I'm not sure I know what you mean," I said.

Lisbet turned away from the mirror. "The first thing I

think of with people is to forgive them. I don't think I'm creative enough to imagine other options." People always talk about how doing the right thing is hard, but Lisbet was the first person whom I'd heard say it's the easiest choice available. Then again, cutting the hair of the guy in my bedroom had always been the easiest option for me.

I turned to leave Lisbet's bathroom. "Remember," she said, "there's something I wanted to ask you too."

"Right."

"You know how I'm getting married next week."

"Of course," I said, though I'd actually forgotten it was the following week.

"I know that you think it's stupid, but you'll still come, right?"

"To your wedding? That's a big deal. It's like your big party. I'm coming to that."

"You said before that you weren't going to come. You said that marriage is an institution for idiots."

"I did not say that." (I'd said that.) "I just meant for some idiots. Not you. You're not an idiot, Lisbet. It's an institution for idiots and non-idiots alike."

"Thank you." Lisbet exhaled and smiled at herself in the mirror. "Do you want to be my maid of honor?"

I looked at Lisbet's face, trying to gauge whether she

was joking, but she wasn't at all. "You haven't asked any-one yet?"

"I was waiting to ask you."

"Why would you want me to be your maid of honor? That's an important job. I mean, maid of honor. That's a really honorable maid. The most honorable maid, some would argue. What about your friends?"

"My friends?"

"Yeah. All your friends."

"I mean, there's Caroline from the yoga studio. And Marcie is in the Marines now, or she would be there. But I guess I don't have a lot of friends. Just Randy. Randy's my best friend."

I thought about Randy and everything I knew about Randy. Sometimes Randy wore a baseball hat. Randy seemed to have a lot of trouble eating prime rib. That was all I knew, and yet he was Lisbet's best friend. I felt very sad for Lisbet. "How can you not have a lot of friends? You're always so happy."

Lisbet smiled very big. "I don't know. So will you do it?"

"Sure . . . "

"Really? Really? Perfect. I don't know if you want to talk about a dress now. No, you have to go to school, right? But maybe I can just give you something to think about, and you can walk around with it for today. Gamboge or ecru? They're both shades of yellow. Oh, and you can bring a date."

"Oh, happiness. Can I really?" I said.

"Weddings are the greatest expressions of love, right? Everyone at a wedding wants to be with someone that they can hopefully feel all that love for. You should bring that tall boy. The one with the wonderful accent and the poems."

"Hmm. Interesting idea." I lifted a perfume bottle from the vanity and held it as if it were a wineglass. "If I drink enough of this perfume, do you think it will poison me to death?"

"Of course," she said. "Why do you ask?"

# CHAPTER 12

# THE NUMBER 10

**N**oah waited for me outside of gym class.

"You know, I never mentioned it, but I thought it was pretty cool you came to Lucy's birthday. She kept saying, 'Can you believe Astrid Krieger came to my birthday party?'"

"Yes, I am wildly exciting."

Noah laughed.

Then he got a little nervous and asked, "Can I walk you to lunch?"

I was about to say, *No, I know how to get there myself, thank you,* but I still didn't know how to get there myself. And surprisingly, I didn't mind the idea of someone walking me. That day, Noah was wearing a blue tuxedo jacket and a grey T-shirt. It took some of the attention off me. And it was way better than walking with Pierre. Noah was very polite in a way that not a lot of people were, particularly Pierre.

"Did you do the homework?" Noah asked as we walked.

"No."

"You don't know which homework I was referring to."

"But I'll save you some time. I didn't do it." If you didn't do your homework at Cadorette, no one seemed to care. The teachers didn't really expect you to do any of the homework, and most of them seemed focused on other things like their divorces. Ninety percent of the teachers at Cadorette had red eyes and couch lines on their faces: telltale signs that their marriages were breaking up.

We walked into the cafeteria. Lunch never changed. The pizza just got older. The indignities piled up. That day, my lunch table wasn't even there. I scanned the crowded cafeteria to check if Summer Wonder's table was now twice as wide. It wasn't, but everyone there was stealing glances at me and laughing, as they tended to do.

"We could sit outside," Noah offered.

"It's raining."

"Yeah." He walked over to the filthy empty space where the table once lived. Lucy carried over her lunch tray and took a seat on the floor as if she wasn't expecting a table to be there in the first place. "Well, are you too good to sit on the floor?" Noah asked with a sly grin.

"Honestly," I said, "I think I am."

"You shouldn't let it bother you," Noah said. Then he too sat on the floor.

"Why shouldn't I? It seems like exactly the kind of thing I should be bothered by." My dress was a fairly complicated collection of purples and greens, lace and buckles. I was very pleased about it when I put it on that morning, but as I hunkered down among the dust bunnies and ants, it felt less like an outfit and more like a contraption. Once I shoved the bulk of it under me, it offered a nice cushion and back support, and the colors were practically blinding against the greys and beiges of the walls and floor. So in that case, it was still successful clothing.

"It could be worse. At my old school, these guys would kick me in the backpack when I walked down the hall. Or someone would lean their hand in from behind my head and flick the back of my ear. It sounds like no big deal, but it hurts."

I felt a damp coldness spread over the top of my legs and looked down to see a wet orange puddle spreading across the fabric over my lap. "Uh," I said. "This is worse."

Noah looked concerned and looked over to Lucy. Lucy said, "Oh . . ."

"What? No. I didn't pee on myself." I reached

underneath my legs. "I sat on my juice box and the straw points up."

They both laughed, but it wasn't a mean laugh. I found it less funny than they did, as I was wet and without a juice box.

Noah looked off to the back of the room as if catching someone's eye. "I'll get you another one," he said, seeming distracted. He walked out in a rush through the far door to the cafeteria—which was in the opposite direction of the place where he could buy another juice box.

I motioned to Lucy. "Follow me."

We stayed a few paces behind Noah as he moved into the hallway. Two guys in black T-shirts—one short, one tall—got behind him really close. Noah took a step. The short one stepped on his heel. And then the tall one smacked Noah on the back of the head. And then the short one hit him again. And Noah just kept walking. He didn't do anything. For the life of me, I could not figure it out. Noah looked pained, like he wished everyone would just stop bothering him. I also wore that expression a lot. It was only when he turned his head and saw me that he acted with any real urgency. He moved quickly and the other guys moved after him but not quickly enough. When Lucy and I turned the corner, Noah and the guys in the black shirts had vanished.

I spun around in a circle to see if someone had dis-appeared behind me, but the hallway had begun to get crowded with people, and I didn't recognize anyone other than Lucy, who was looking at me anxiously as if await-ing instruction. "Lucy, do you know how I told you I had a skill for figuring out how someone is useful?"

"Yes," she said.

"Well, didn't you wonder how you're useful?"

"Sure. That'd be nice to know."

If I were inclined toward honesty, I'd tell Lucy that she was just about as useful as a carrot in a knife fight. I couldn't say that, but I wasn't going to lie to her either. She did have a particular talent. "It's information," I said.

"Information?"

"You know who everyone is and what everyone does. No one can make a plan without information. It's very valuable." Of course, she was completely useless at observ-ing anything that happened to herself—not only was she still eating her hair, but there was a scab on her arm that she couldn't leave the hell alone—but I couldn't expect her to be perfect.

"Very valuable?" she asked hopefully.

"For instance, I actually need some information now. So I've come to the right place."

Lucy was giddy. "Go. Ask me anything."

"Who were those guys smacking Noah around the hall?"

"I don't know," she said. I wiped my closed eyes, trying hard to not show my annoyance.

"Information. Think, Lucy. This is how you're useful."

"Sorry. This has been happening. I think some people just don't like Noah."

"Yes, but why?"

"I don't know. There are people who like to make things hard for new kids at Cadorette."

"Yes, I'm aware. I just tried to eat lunch on the floor, and the entire lower half of my body is covered in juice. But why Noah?"

"I heard someone say he looks like the 1970s threw up on his shirt."

"Yeah," I said. "That was me."

"He's just different. You're different too. People don't like that. It makes them mad."

"Who were the guys following him? Who's the short guy with the long chestnut hair like a lovely pony? The one wearing a black T-shirt with Satan leading a line of people into a meat grinder?"

Lucy thought about it for a moment, weighing ideas. "His name is Lance, but people call him Melty."

"Because of his skin?"

"He likes to melt things."

"Of course. And the other one? Tall with curly hair?"

She paused for a moment. "I don't know," she said, but something in her tone told me she couldn't be believed.

"I'm serious, Lucy. I already know what he looks like."

"If I tell you, are you going to hurt him?"

"I don't know. I haven't made a plan yet."

"Promise you won't do anything bad to him?"

"Lucy, I don't think you understand. I *have* to do something bad to him. Otherwise, no one will." I sighed. "Lucy, do you even know why I'm here?"

She blinked a bunch of times. "Like, because of . . . God?"

"No, do you know why I'm in this school?"

"Uh-uh."

"I used to go to the Bristol Academy. You know that, right?"

"Yeah."

"And I got kicked out. Okay? And it was because someone went behind my back and betrayed me."

"I thought it was because you cheated?"

"Yes. Kind of. But cheating is a complicated issue. If you had the opportunity to ask any athlete, politician, businessperson, or celebrity you really like if cheating ever helped them succeed, do you know what they would say?"

"No?" Lucy said.

"Exactly. And that would be a lie. And lying is just another form of cheating. I would still be at Bristol if someone hadn't betrayed me. And that's not right. People can't just get away with messing with people like me or you or Noah. So, I'm here to make stuff like that right, okay? And if you tell me who he is, I can take care of him. It's the right thing to do."

"But you know what he looks like."

"Revenge takes research and understanding. A little information is never as good as a lot of information."

"Okay. I understand. But I just need you to promise you won't hurt him."

Lucy wasn't ever going to understand me. It just wasn't her way. And it was very easy for me to make promises because promises were the sorts of things that you could make up and down all the livelong day, if you had no intention of keeping them. I'm positive that I promised my parents when I was thirteen that I would never curse again. Can you believe that shit?

But Lucy had caught me at a new point in my life. I was waist deep in the middle of Dean Rein's challenge. I was now trying to keep promises. "Whoever it is," I said, "I won't hurt him."

Lucy nodded. "His name is Mason."

"What's the deal with him?" I said.

"He's . . . he's artistic."

"He's autistic?"

"I don't know," she said. "Maybe. He painted that."

Lucy pointed to the end of the hallway, where a mural hung. It read: *Nominate Your Homecoming King and Queen.* The painting was of a vengeful and angry king and queen standing above their fallen enemies, bloody swords in hand. The king held the heart of one of his victims. Noah's two torturers really liked bloody, dead people. I then noticed that Lucy had adopted a dreamy look when talking about Mason. It was a look I recognized from movies, similar to how Talia Pasteur looked at Pierre or Lisbet's dog looked at things he was going to pee on. Lucy and Mason would make a weird couple. I would've guessed Lucy would like someone exactly like herself, but admittedly I never totally understood love. I shouldn't have been surprised, though. Vivi ended up with my father even though she was born outside a hippie commune on the floor of a Volkswagen van, while my father literally grew up with a silver spoon in his mouth—so he would always know where it was when it was time to eat cereal or soup. Mason was very long and thin, while Lucy was short and squat. Together they would look exactly like the number 10. Well, more like the number 1o. But I couldn't give their potential coupling careful consideration just then. I'd become distracted by the homecoming nomination mural. It wasn't because I had any real interest in homecoming kings and queens. I was interested because of what was under the mural. "Hey," I yelled across the hallway, "that's my lunch table."

The boy behind the table wore a T-shirt for some band he was glad no one had ever heard of. The Laundry Children? The Scoliosis Twins? Something like that. The paper hanging in front of his seat at the table said that he was the student council president. Also, he was named Ben. The paper said that too.

"You stole my lunch table," I said. "I had to sit on the floor."

"This is a school table. It could be from anywhere."

"Yes," I said, "but I was the one who carved 'Cadorette High School Sucks' right there."

Ben shook his head. "That could've been anyone."

"I don't think just anyone carves with such ornate calligraphy."

"You may have a point. I'm sorry. I could give it back, but the lunch period is almost over. Perhaps you'd like to nominate someone for homecoming court instead. Because you're here and all."

I hadn't given the homecoming dance much thought. I didn't care about any of that stuff. We didn't have homecoming at Bristol. We instead had something called Boat Days. But I was interested in the concept of homecoming queen. It had nothing to do with dresses or dancing or feeling special on the inside and outside and all that worthless crap. Pretty much, I just wanted everyone in the school to understand that I was Astrid Krieger, for godssake. I wanted people to understand what that meant. A position of royalty seemed like a good first step.

"Tell me," I said, "this homecoming queen, does the title come with its own tiara?"

He leaned back in his chair, barely bothering to look at me. "There's a thing the queen wears on her head. Yeah."

"Platinum?"

"I'm sure it's plastic."

"I'm sure I could bring my own. And the throne? Do they just keep it at the front of the school and people move it around, or is there one in each classroom that the queen attends?"

He wasn't sure if I was serious or not. "Homecoming queen is just for the dance and the football game."

"Hmm . . . So, they can't really issue edicts throughout the school year or anything?"

"No." He held his hand open. "It's a dollar a nomination."

"Well, how much to ensure that I actually win?"

He was a little bit troubled by the question. "I don't know. It'll just get you on the ballot. Five dollars. Twenty dollars. It goes into the dance fund, and anything above that goes to the extracurriculars. Did you know that there's a literary magazine . . . " I stopped listening and reached into my purse. There was a nice roll of bills about the size of my fist. I was positive it was enough.

"That all sounds neat," I said. "I would like five hundred nominations."

"Uh, all on you, or would you like to spread this out on anyone else?"

I hadn't really thought it through, but good deeds could be found anywhere.

"It's interesting," I said to Ben. "It's as if you already know about my challenge." I might have been making things too hard for myself. I could do good *and* reap life's rewards at the same time. But at that moment, I saw Melty and Mason. I turned back to Ben, perhaps a little too excited. "Yes!" I told him. "Spread it!"

I walked over to Noah's enemies and stood in their way. "Excuse me. Excuse me? Sirs?" I said. I must've sounded like a weirdo. No one under the age of fifty expects to be called "sir." "So, I've been issued a challenge to do good things. Retribution for your crimes would be viewed by most as a very good deed." I knew Dean Rein wouldn't count it, but no one else needed to know that.

This was just too much for Melty to understand. He grunted a kind of "Wheh?" They walked around me. Or at least they tried to, but I cut them off.

"I know Noah, and I don't want you to bother him. Okay?"

Melty said, "Okay," but he was smiling in a knowing way, and it did not sound like he meant it.

I stuck my hand in my purse. In most states, you can only buy pepper spray that's just ten percent the actual ingredient that causes pain. I find this unacceptable. If it's legal, then it isn't going to serve its purpose. A guy who lives on the sheep farm near Bristol had been getting me some really major stuff from Indonesia.

"I'm very serious and you leave me no choice," I said, spraying Melty in the face. It looked like it really hurt. I mean, bad. Melty yelled that it hurt like a "Jesus mother faaaaaaa." That sounded about right.

Mason's eyes were wide with real terror. I have no idea how he would've described the pain had he been subjected to it like Melty. I almost wish I could've known because he would've probably described it visually, since he's a painter. But I didn't spray him. I had made a promise to Lucy. And I was someone who (as of about twenty minutes ago) always kept her promises. I held the pepper spray up to his face and he squinted and flinched, but he didn't run away and I didn't spray. I just said, "Pow." And then I said, "Nothing. You don't get sprayed. And now you owe me a favor."

Melty was running down the hall, blindly trying to find a bathroom or some other place of refuge. I yelled after him, "I'm Astrid Krieger. I would like to be your homecoming queen."

Ben was watching the whole thing. I think he took the job of student council president a little too seriously, even though like homecoming queen, it's not a job with any sort of power. "There's a zero tolerance policy on weapons in this school. If you're caught, they'll kick you out."

"Really? That would be amazing." Unfortunately, I was never caught and strangely, even the people who hated me didn't tell on me. In that way and many others, high school was a lot like prison.

I wasn't sure if Noah would still want to walk me from

my classes—I thought maybe he'd be embarrassed after the Melty-Mason incident—but when he met me outside my US History class, it made me happy. I felt like I did a pretty good thing for Noah. It wasn't on the level of feeding poor children with cancer, but it was something. A piece of something that was going to be bigger. But I still had a lot more I needed to do for him.

"Well," I said.

"Well, what?"

"Those guys are never going to bother you again. Are you going to thank me?"

"Am I going to thank you?" he asked with a tinge of disbelief.

"Yeah. Did you see what I did just now?"

Noah scrunched up his face and shuffled back a little, apparently uncomfortable.

"You *should* thank me." I handed him one of my business cards. Everyone should have business cards.

He looked at it. He had no idea what he was supposed to do with it. "My home address is on the back," I said. "Or if you get lost, just look for the biggest house. The biggest house ever. Be there at eight. I have a plan."

He didn't say anything. He just kept looking at the card.

ASTRID KRIEGER

"I like to make business cards."

1 Great Cormorant Drive

Cadorette Township, Connecticut

(Please, no phone calls, email, or menus. Thank you.)

# CHAPTER 13

# THE ROCKET SHIP

**N**oah was supposed to come at eight, but I spotted him hovering around the driveway of the main house at about seven twenty.

"Why are you here?" I asked.

"I had no idea how long it would take me to get to here."

I considered leaving him there for forty minutes (because he shouldn't have assumed I had nothing to do with the early part of my evening), but I decided that would be lousy of me. "It's this way to my room," I said, leading him across the main lawn.

"You really do live in a rocket ship," he commented when we got there.

"You didn't believe me?" I closed the hatch behind him.

"It's not that I didn't believe you. It's just . . . people

don't normally live in rocket ships. This couldn't be legal to own, could it?" Noah didn't really know where to sit. Instead, he stood at this weird, hunched angle in order to avoid hitting his head.

"Of course it's illegal," I said. "But everyone does it."

"Everyone owns a rocket ship and lives in it?"

"It's more common than you think."

"I'm sure you're the only person in the world who does."

"What about astronauts?"

"They technically don't live in rocket ships while they're in the world."

"You make an okay point." I sat down on the bed and indicated that Noah should sit in the bucket seat next to the bed.

I took a juice box out of the small refrigerator on the other side of the bed and squeezed the whole thing into my mouth until my cheeks were really big. Then I swallowed it in a single gulp. I fished around for the last drops by blowing the box up like a balloon, then squeezing it flat. This was a thing I did all the time. It's pretty much the only way I drink things—at least things that are in box form. I probably would never have known that this was kind of weird if I hadn't looked at Noah's face just then.

"You've seen me drink these at school," I said.

"I guess I hadn't really watched the whole process." He looked like he was staring at one of those optical illusions that you see on menus: *Are you looking at a picture of a princess or an old woman or an old princess?*

"I'm sorry," I said. "I forgot to ask you if you wanted one."

"I think I'm off juice . . . " he said.

"It's not disgusting. I promise. They actually stopped making this flavor, and what's in my refrigerator might actually be the last of its kind in the entire world. I have no idea why more people wouldn't want limeade in a box. I'm much happier to have it all to myself."

"I think we're all happier this way," he said.

"Look," I said. "About today. I helped you out. And I'm glad I did. But now I need something from you."

Noah tilted his head back and looked skyward. Then he took his wallet out of his back pocket. It was Velcro and made out of parachute material. *Really?* I thought. *And you're not nine years old?* He pulled out a small collection of crumpled bills. "I don't have a lot of money or anything. I just carry a few bucks." He handed them over and I instinctively grabbed for them (it's hard to change who you are), but then I let go.

"I don't need any money. That's not what I meant."

"No, it's fair. Fifteen bucks per spray per face. That's thirty dollars total."

"What I need is—"

"I'm gonna stop you there, Astrid. It's all I have on me. And frankly, it's all I'm willing to pay you."

"No. You're not getting it. This is what I need: I need you to let me fix you," I said.

"Fix me?" He looked at me to make sure he heard me right. "Wow. Thanks." He didn't say this like you would if someone gave you a birthday present and you're pretending you don't want it when you actually do. He said it like you would if you really didn't want the birthday present. Like, if it wasn't a present at all. Just a box full of cat skulls.

"I think I can really help you."

"Why do I need help?"

"Why? I mean, it's pretty obvious. You see yourself, right?" I pointed to the mirror on my desk area. "Sociopaths hit you in the head. I saw it happen. And you don't do anything. Nothing."

"Why do you think I do nothing?"

"Are you scared?"

"No. I'm not scared. I just refuse. If you hit back, it gets worse. And then you never stop fighting."

"You can't be like you forever," I said. "There's going

to be something worth fighting for and then you won't even know what to do."

He said, "Yeah, but you can't be like you forever either. Someday, you're going to have to *stop* fighting everyone." I had thought he would pretty much be in favor of whatever I wanted him to do, but he didn't even let me tell him what that was. I was offering to fix him, and I was pretty much expecting him to say, "Yes!"

I even pictured him doing one of those scenes you see in movies, where the dopey but amiable protagonist tries on outfit after outfit in a clothing store, and after, like, the first fifteen times he walks out of the dressing room, I shake my head. But then the last time I nod and give him a thumbs-up. We were going to do that. In real life.

Instead, he told me that he didn't want me to fix him and that I was the one who needed to be fixed. It's kind of funny because him just saying that proved that I had already changed a little bit. If someone said to me a few months before, *"You can't be like you forever,"* I would have given him a permanent click in his jaw. But maybe it was the way Noah said it. He wasn't trying to say the meanest thing he could think of. He was matter-of-fact and unemotional about it, like he was telling me some sort of stupid fact about penguins or something. Like he was offhandedly mentioning that a penguin's stomach will explode if it eats just one cashew nut. (Don't quote me on that. It's probably not a true fact.)

I didn't feel angry, like I normally would if someone said anything critical about me. Instead, I realized he was right. "Yup, that's true. I can't be like this forever."

"Have you considered the possibility that I don't do anything to change myself because I don't *want* to do anything?" he asked.

"No," I said. "I have not considered that."

Noah smiled and relaxed a little bit. "I didn't . . . I didn't mean to say that in a bad way. I was just saying that you're looking at me, and you see someone who lets things happen to him, right?"

"Well, yeah. And I also see someone who dresses like he runs an illegal dice game out of a car wash in 1974 and his name is something like 'Frankie the Weasel.'"

"That's very specific."

"I've been thinking about it all week."

"Okay," he said. "But all that, who I am and what I look like—that's a choice. It's my choice. And no, it may not always be the best choice. But . . . but I look at you and then I see . . . I don't know."

"What? What do you see when you look at me? I can take it, you know," I went on after he hesitated. "I'm not a particularly sensitive person or anything. I'm not going to cry."

"I know. I wasn't saying that you're sensitive. In fact, I know you're not."

"Well, let's not get carried away. I could be more sensitive than you think. I'm not, but it's possible."

"The thing is, I look at you and I just have no idea at all. I've been trying to figure you out. But I can't. You know how when we were in the nurse's office and I said I'd heard about you before? It wasn't . . . I heard you got in trouble a lot, but I didn't hear you were mean or anything."

"But I am mean," I said.

Noah smiled, which was a weird reaction to someone insisting they're mean.

"I am mean," I said again. "I'll prove it. Guess what? You're going to probably be bald someday."

"Probably. All of my grandparents are bald. I have a bald grandma. She wears bright orange wigs."

"I can do better than that," I told him.

"But I know there's more to you, Astrid," he said. "I know when I look at you. I can tell when you ask me a question that you're waiting to hear what I have to say. Most people just wait for their turn to speak."

"Really? What would give you the impression I'm not like most people?"

"You are certainly not most people. When have you ever waited your turn to do anything?"

And then the night felt easy. We sat on top of the nose of the rocket under the stars, so it looked like we were in the middle of space and about to die because you can't sit on top of a rocket ship in space in your regular clothes. I didn't usually like to tell people much about myself. (This, you have to understand, was before I decided to write a whole stupid book where I have so far done nothing but tell people about myself.) I talked about Bristol and Dean Rein and therapy and why I had to go to Cadorette, all the way up to Dean Rein's challenge to do good things. Finally I explained why I thought that fixing Noah would be a good thing. When I was finished, I thought about how weird the whole challenge must have sounded out loud. I was sure Noah was like all the other people who didn't have to think about doing good things. It just sort of came to them as naturally as walking and having lunch.

When I finished, though, he didn't ask about the challenge. He was interested in something else entirely. "Why would you want to go back to Bristol?" he wanted to know.

"What do you mean?" I thought it was pretty obvious, but maybe it wasn't if you were used to schools like Cadorette, where the textbooks were covered in gum and bathroom walls listed which girls had the biggest breasts—in 1987. The map in my social studies class only had forty-eight states. "Cadorette Township High School's a dump," I said.

"Yeah. I mean, I'm not saying I like it there either, but what's so great about the old place? Other than all the rich people?"

I tried to put it into terms he could understand. "You know how in the Harry Potter movies where he has all of these magic powers at his magic school, but if he wasn't at his magic school, he wouldn't have the powers anymore?"

"That's not actually how Harry Potter works. He always has the—"

"I really don't care. That's not the point. The point is what you're seeing right here. This Astrid Krieger you see in front of you . . . she's not me. I'm much different than what you've seen. I'm just . . . I'm usually very powerful." This was a hard idea for him to wrap his head around, but he didn't ask any follow-up questions about the Bristol Astrid vs. the current Astrid. Maybe he found me pretty powerful already, and he didn't need any convincing. After all, he had come all the way out to my house without me having to coerce him.

"I will have a juice, after all. Unless you have water," he said.

I handed him a juice box. "Water doesn't taste like anything," I said.

He drank it slowly, missing the point of the juice box entirely. When he was done, he got around to what he was trying to say the whole time. "I think I understand. I understand you want to be powerful. But we only have about six months left of high school."

"Right."

"So then what?"

"So then what, what?"

"Are you staying here?"

"With my family, never."

"Do you like your family?"

"I like my grandfather. Lisbet's nice."

"Do you like your parents?"

"Does anyone like their parents?"

"I like my parents."

"Well, you're either a weirdo or you don't know your father has, like, another family somewhere with his mistress and secret children."

"My parents aren't married anymore. He doesn't have secret children. He has actual public children with my stepmother. I still like him, though."

"I'm sure he'll let you down eventually."

"How are you so sure?"

"Because he's a person. And people let people down."

"That's, uh . . . You're really cynical."

"Have we met? I'm super cynical."

"Did you ever like your parents?"

"My dad's harmless. He was just always more into Lisbet. They would play tennis or go deer hunting. They never actually shot a deer, and Lisbet never wanted to hold the hunting rifle because it was heavy, but they liked wearing hunting jackets. So Vivi and I would spend those days doing the sorts of things Vivi liked to do. We would sit in mud and buy shoes and have high tea at the Plaza. We liked each other."

"So then what happened?"

"She wanted more. She wanted more people around who loved her. She probably should've just gotten another dog. But instead, she had my brother. They named him Frederick, but everyone called him Fritz, which was the dog's name."

"I didn't know you had a brother."

"Why would you? No one talks about him very much anymore."

"You and your brother aren't close?"

"We were really close. I loved my brother, like more than I loved anyone. He had dark hair like me. We dark-haired kids were like a separate team. I convinced him that we were adopted from the same birth parents—a family of coal miners from West Virginia. Most kids would be really upset if they thought they were adopted, but Fritz liked the mystery. I told him the coal-mining McNutters were raising eight kids, but they had eight more that they had to farm out elsewhere. They could only afford every other kid, and so they sold the extras to rich families, and Vivi paid a million dollars for each of us. Also, the McNutters were descended from gypsies, and they practiced black magic, and one of our long-lost siblings was a serial killer from Texas known as the Alphabet Slasher. It's hard to find a lot of five-year-olds who would laugh at a story about a long-lost brother who stabs prostitutes in alphabetical order, but Fritz was a good kid. And then Vivi got really angry when she heard about our stories and she was like, 'If you were adopted, Astrid, please explain this.' Then she lifted the bottom of her blouse and showed off her cesarean scar. So I told Fritz, 'The Alphabet Slasher strikes again.'"

I started laughing at the story because it was one of my favorites, but when I looked over at Noah, he put his hand gently on my shoulder. "What happened to Fritz, Astrid?"

"He died. He drowned when he was five."

"I'm sorry."

"Yeah, me too. It was my fault."

"No, that's not fair. Of course it wasn't your fault. You were a kid."

"Yeah," I said. "It's not fair. Let's go somewhere, okay?" I slid off the rocket ship. "I'm not opposed to the idea of ice cream."

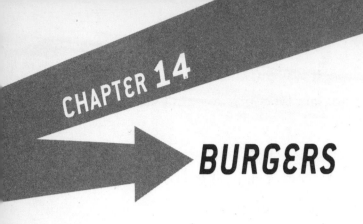

# CHAPTER 14

# BURGERS

**N**oah drove up Route 7 until we found a fast-food restaurant. There was no actual indoor part to the place,
except where they cooked the food. It was a restaurant,
but you had to stay in your car. I'd never been to one.
Noah was incredulous.

"You've never been to this one?" he said.

And I said, "No. I've never been to *any* one. Not this
chain of restaurants. Not any other fast-food place. Ever."
My grandfather hated fast food. He described the concept
as "the unwashed masses served with unwashed hands."

That the whole country was filled with food served
fast and I'd never experienced it was the craziest thing
Noah had ever heard. "But you eat horrible food all the
time. I've seen you," he said.

"I know," I agreed. "But you can get horrible food
anywhere. Even nice places."

There was a large board with the menu on it on the

outside of the restaurant. I was kind of shocked by how cheap everything was. I'd been to lots of convenience stores and was even arrested for robbing one (or two or seven, misunderstandings all), but I'd never thought you could get an entire meal for three dollars. It was more expensive at the school cafeteria. I could buy a burger for everyone parked at the restaurant with one bill from my wallet, and not even the largest bill.

I pressed the button on the menu board that said *Press here to order*, but nothing happened. There was just a pop of white noise coming out of the speaker. I waved over a boy about my age. He was wearing a paper hat and an apron covered in ketchup, like he just murdered someone in the kitchen.

"How does this work?" I asked.

"Um, here's a list of food that we have. Here are the prices. And then you pick the food that you want, and then you say what you want, and then you pay me, and then I bring the food," the guy in the apron said.

"No. I know how a menu works. How do you order into this thing?" But that even confused the guy more. "Forget it. I want a vanilla milk shake, a large water for the missus—"

"Thanks," Noah said.

"And french fries and um . . . twenty-three burgers."

"Twenty-three? Two-three?"

"Two-three."

Noah and I didn't want to sit in the car because not being cramped was the exact reason that we had left my home in the first place. We tried to sit on the hood of the car, but it buckled under our weight, so we sat on the curb in front of the car instead.

"You know," Noah said, "buying all of these people burgers probably isn't really a good deed. It's not like it's going to help them. It's just a treat."

"But it's not a bad thing, is it?"

"No. It isn't."

"I'm going to count it."

A familiar car was parked three spaces away from us in the parking lot. The voices coming from the car were also familiar. I could hear some laughter and snippets of my name and references to Noah, whom they were calling "Spaz Face." I figured that this was the sort of place where the kids from Cadorette liked to drive and yell things at each other. It was probably popular for the same reason that we were there in the first place—because if you kept on driving, you'd eventually find it. Noah and I must have made for an interesting couple, but the sound of their laughter didn't make my face feel hot like it had before. The hot face must have come from feeling out of place, and I wasn't out of place. I liked talking with Noah. And Noah never cared about people laughing.

"Sometimes, people don't realize high school isn't forever," Noah said. "But things will of course be okay later."

"How do you figure?"

"Because soon I'll be doing what I want to do."

"And what's that?" I asked.

I could tell he was choosing his words carefully. I think he worried I was going to make fun of him. "I want to be a journalist." He took a sip of his water and waited. When I didn't say anything, he stared at me. "You have no opinion on my career aspirations, Astrid?"

"Nope," I said. "I don't read."

"It's what I've always wanted to do. I used to look at newspapers before I could even really understand them. I would figure out the connections between the words and the pictures. I liked it. I liked how words made me feel."

I didn't really want to laugh at him, but that was funny, so I couldn't help it. "You must have had so many friends. They'd come over. You'd talk about how words felt."

"I think we both know that didn't happen too much," he said.

"Yes. Duh."

"You must have felt that way about . . . What are you passionate about?" He looked at my face for some sort of clue, but I was careful not to give anything away. "Hitting people?"

"No. Lots of things. I don't know."

"Are you going to college?" he wanted to know.

"I don't know."

"Have you applied?"

"Why? Is it hard to get into college?"

"Sometimes. For some people."

"Not for someone like me, though. Is that what you're saying?"

Noah looked like he was trying not to say anything that would make me mad. "My parents weren't good with money," he said. "It's my responsibility to find a way to do it for myself. It's hard. I don't like it. I'm not saying there's anything wrong with being like you, but you don't have to worry about it. Your family's full of all those oil barons and senators."

"And a princess," I said.

"What?"

"My great-great-aunt was the princess of Austria."

"Right. Anyway, it's been harder for me than I wish. Even if I get in somewhere, I need a scholarship."

And then our food came.

I knew what Noah was trying to say, and I knew he thought that I didn't often consider my future after high school (whichever high school it happened to be), but of course I did. However, when I thought about my future, it was a lot more about what I didn't want than what I wanted.

My parents were happy with Lisbet and her life, so that was probably what they wanted for me too. Living at home, marrying some guy, and soon enough having roughly three babies named Satchel, Jerushah, and Gretel (this is what Lisbet planned on naming her eventual children). When I pictured my future, I didn't picture a husband. I definitely didn't picture children, and I didn't have names for them (other than Childrens Krieger, of course).

I thought about my grandfather and how powerful he was, and there was something to that. I liked that if he wanted something, he didn't have to change the world to get it. The world changed for him. If that doesn't make sense to you, then you probably will never be a powerful person. Nobody ever told my grandfather how he should behave or what he should or shouldn't think. If he wanted something, people found a way to give it to him. It all goes back to that painting: "Never let anyone stop you from having everything you want."

That concept appealed to me. But my grandfather had always said that to be like him, I would have to be exactly like him. Live his life over, basically. Like him, I went to

Bristol. But I wasn't interested in the rest of his life. Like him, he would want me to go to Harvard, then join the navy, then work for the family business, and then run for Senate. It was a source of frustration that, since I was a female and it was not 1943, it would be impossible for me to kill as many Japanese as he did in World War II. "There were no dames on my PT boat," he would say. "I'm not saying it's impossible, but to do it right, you'll need a time machine and a sex change."

As for college? I didn't know. I knew I didn't want to work for Krieger Industries—partially because none of the employees ever really looked like they wanted to be there, and also I'd never been interested in making things designed to blow people up. I'm by no means a people person, but I'm also not a dead-people person. When I thought about my future, I didn't have all the details, but it looked something like this:

"I like New York as a city," I said. "I like cities in general. And I have never lived in one. I like that everything is right there in a city, but you can also stay inside and shut the door and be alone. I imagine a big apartment, but I actually don't need it to be that big. When my mother calls, I won't have to answer. I could even change my name so nobody could find me, though I like 'Astrid Krieger,' so I probably won't follow through on that. I would have the food I want. The TV I want. The geography I want. And no one else will bother me about anything. I imagine that sort of life as happy. Well, maybe not happy, but better."

"Isn't that more or less what you have right now?"

"No. Now I have to live here and go to school."

"What you're talking about isn't a future," Noah said. "Maybe that's an afternoon, but it's not enough. And it's actually kind of sad."

"Sorry," I said. "But it's my plan for me. You can do whatever you want."

"But what about friends?"

"I have no use for friends. Never have."

"What about me?" he said. "Are we friends?" Writing it down, it sounds a little desperate, but it didn't sound that way then.

"I don't know. Maybe."

"What about a job? You have to have a job."

"I don't have to have a job."

"Eventually, you do."

"Why?"

"Because that's what people do. This place is hiring." He pointed to a Help Wanted sign affixed to the kitchen. The sign showed a smiling milk shake filling out an application.

"I think I'm more qualified for something that couldn't

be done by a milk shake with eyes. Plus, that milk shake looks just like the milk shake on the sign. That's obviously how he got the job."

"Yeah," he said. "Nepotism."

>>>>>>>>>>>>>

The burgers didn't look very much like their picture, but that probably explained why they were only a dollar. They looked like brown mush in between white mush. But even at their best, that's kind of what burgers are. The boy in the paper hat gave them to me in three white bags, and I passed them out. There were truck drivers and old men and a mother with a little girl and everyone was more than happy to have a free burger. Well, maybe not happy. More like confused. But they were willing to take them. And that's sort of like happiness.

The car with all the laughing was different. Of course, there was the red-faced kid with the beer shirt. And there was another guy who was just in a wrestling onesie. And there was a skinny girl with slumped shoulders and sunglasses that she was wearing even though it was nighttime. And another girl with a face of freckles and big hair. And of course Summer Wonder was there, as it was her car.

"The two of you make a beautiful couple," she said to

me and Noah when I walked up to her car. And she said it
in such a way as to ensure we knew that she didn't mean
a single word of the sentence. I even doubted the "two of
you" part, for a second. Like, maybe there were suddenly
three of us. Her tone was that opposite from what she
really meant.

But I looked at Noah, and I didn't feel bad about being
with him at all. "Burger?" I offered.

Summer looked at her friends, then back to me. "What
did you do to it?"

"Nothing. That's just how they make burgers here."

"I don't want your burger," she said. But when she
looked back at her friends for the second time, there
appeared to be a mutiny.

"They're free?" Beer Shirt asked.

I nodded.

"Sweet," he said, dipping his hand in the bag. "Can I
have two?" He took two, then pulled one out for everyone
else in the car.

Summer Wonder looked at her burger in a cunning
way, like she was going to mash it up and wipe it in my
hair in a repeat of the Twinkie incident, but then she
didn't. She didn't say "Thanks," but she ate the burger. It
was a small victory.

I finished my milk shake as Noah drove me back to

my place. It was there in the car that I had an idea. "You know," I told him, "what I'm doing right now could actually be my job."

"Which part?" he said.

"Like when I gave out the burgers. I could do that. But for a living."

"That's not really a job. That would cost money."

"Not every job is for money. I could be like a charity person or the pope, but on a slightly smaller scale."

"You know, a lot of people do good things all the time. But they do other things for jobs."

"Not like me, though. I'm going to do it so much better. I'm going to do a really good job. A great job."

"And you're going to help people in need, or you're still going to try to fix me?"

"Oh, you're in need," I said. "You are in desperate need."

Noah laughed a little, but I could tell he wasn't positive whether I was making a joke. (I wasn't.) "What are you going to do?"

"It's what you are going to do. Do you want to come with me to my sister's wedding? It's on Saturday."

"How is that going to fix me?" he asked, smiling.

"It's not. I'm the maid of honor, so I have to go. But if you come with me, I won't have to talk to anyone stupid."

"Yes. I'd love to," he said.

"Good. Wear a suit or something. But not something velvet or from a thrift store. A real suit. I know a tailor, if you need one."

"I'll manage," he said. "And as a bonus, we'll have something to do on Saturday. So no homecoming dance."

"Nope," I said. "We have to go there too."

"What for?"

"Isn't it obvious? I have a plan."

# CHAPTER 15

# CREAM-FILLED DAYS

Once I began thinking of doing good things like it was a job, it was a lot easier. Clients didn't need to find me. I found them. Lucy was an obvious choice. She arguably needed the most help of anyone. And I mean anyone in the world.

Lucy and I were lab partners in Biology. This was an ideal arrangement because if Lucy was going to do all the work anyway, she might as well be sitting next to me. At Bristol, we had dissected a fetal pig. I think they were probably dissecting a cat the next year. Dissecting animals certainly fell under my strict *I don't want to do anything* rule, but then again, I had always enjoyed doing things that made other people uncomfortable. Pierre had been my lab partner at Bristol. He'd started crying as soon as the scalpel touched the pig skin. "He had so much more to give this world," Pierre cried. It was kind of hilarious.

Fetal pigs were way too fancy for Cadorette. I mean,

they probably cost as much as three dollars, and that wasn't in the budget. Cadorette couldn't even afford real condiments. In biology classes, we dissected worms. Since there weren't enough, Lucy and I had to wait for someone else's used worm. This gave Lucy and me a chance to really discuss her problem. "Let's talk," I suggested, seizing the opportunity.

"How can I help you, Astrid?" Lucy said. There was a big smile on her face.

"No. I'm here to help *you*."

"With what?"

"I'm going to help you with you."

"With my what?" With her hair in her mouth and her lisp, it clearly sounded like she said, "Itch my butt."

"That," I told her, "is precisely the problem. I'm going to ask you some questions, and I want you to answer them honestly, okay?"

Lucy nodded.

"And for the sake of time and my tendency to get headaches, try to answer these questions with as little as possible obstructing your mouth," I said.

Lucy was lost for a moment, so I pointed to the hair in her gullet. When I was met with no real reaction, I very slowly pulled it out. She reacted as someone who has just spontaneously lost her sight but was too polite to say anything about it. It was obvious that this wasn't going to work, so I signaled with my finger that she could put the hair back. She was thrilled.

My questions were designed to find out what Lucy needed the most help with and who she really was. But her answers were indecipherable. She told me that when she was a kid, she dreamed of one day growing up to be "what a twin Aryan Aztec isn't." I had her repeat it seven times. It was only after I wrote this part of the book and sent her an email that I figured out what the hell she was talking about. Can you figure it out? The answer is revealed at the end of the chapter.*

The strangest thing about Lucy was that she didn't want to change. She didn't want to stop eating her hair. She didn't want to speak in a way that made her coherent. She didn't want to dress better. She didn't even care that much anymore about being what a twin Aryan Aztec isn't.

"I want to be in love," Lucy said.

"Just that?"

"*Just that?*" she repeated, incredulous. "That's everything."

Lucy stood up to get a handout on worm stomachs, but I stopped her. "I'll get it," I said, in the interest of doing another good thing.

I felt bad for Lucy. Lucy thought love was everything.

And that was sad because she probably only knew about love from books about vampires. I figured that finding love for Lucy would be easy. Although, I really didn't know anyone who was in love. My mother and father definitely didn't love each other. He needed someone to talk to, and she needed him to pay for things. That's not love. Lisbet couldn't possibly love Randy. I would say that she loved the idea of Randy, whatever that was. I loved my grandfather, but that was more of a mutual respect than the sort of love most people feel for family. Still, he was the only person in my whole life for whom I felt anything resembling love—other than my brother, Fritz.

And that wasn't the kind of love Lucy was asking for anyway. Lucy didn't want the kind of love between a grandfather and a granddaughter or a brother and a sister. Lucy wanted someone she could kiss and hold hands with and take to a homecoming dance.

By the time I picked up the worksheet and returned to the table, a used worm was ready for us. It was all cut up and basically worthless.

"It looks like it spells something."

It did. The mangled parts of the worm were made to look like letters. And those letters read ASTRID, WHY! And then in worm guts it said underneath *My place 5:00.* I knew what it meant and who left it there. It wasn't a mystery. The writer of the worm note was not very smart. Still, perhaps he could be useful.

"Do you still want to go to the homecoming dance, Lucy?" I asked.

Her eyes got big, and her smile grew wide enough to cause her hair to fall out of her mouth, though she was quick to remedy that. She nodded.

"I'll take care of it. I'll find you a date."

"Really? You know a boy who would want to go with me?"

"More or less," I said.

>>>>>>>>>>>>>

When Pierre left the Bristol Academy, he moved into a furnished apartment in a complex just next to the border of Cadorette Township and Cadorette Village. The complex was split into brick buildings, each holding six units. Most of the people who lived there were single mothers and recently divorced men who had run out of money. It was easy to discover which apartment was Pierre's. It was the only one with a bright orange Ferrari Scuderia with a license plate that said BLAYZZZIN! parked outside.

Pierre was home. He was obviously waiting for me. He'd been staging a whole scene for me beginning with the note made of worms. He stood on a stool in the middle of the room. A poorly tied noose made from either bedsheets or T-shirts was tied around his neck. You'd probably need to actually know Pierre to know what it all looked like. Pierre was acting. He'd done pretty much the same thing with different tools at least seven other times. He had walked in front of cars and swallowed as many as six children's Tylenol in my presence, and yet he remained very much alive.

"I need you to do something for me," I said.

"You read my worm," he said. Pierre concentrated very hard on making a single, solitary tear fall down his cheek. "But it is too late. I am in the middle of doing something."

I did my best impression of fear and concern (the same amount of concern one might have for a broken nail—but a second-tier nail, like the left ring finger). "No. Please. Don't," I said.

Pierre wiped away his tear. He was reasonably satisfied.

"I need you to do something for me," I said again.

"What?"

"I want you to go to the homecoming dance."

This time, he cried a genuine tear. It was embarrassing for both of us. "You want me to go to the homecoming dance with you? Astrid, I cannot say I have felt any emotion deeper than I feel right—"

"Not with me. You misunderstood. I have a date."

"You want me to go to the homecoming dance, but not with you?"

"I need you to go with Lucy Hair Eater."

"Why? And I hope it is a reason greater than a desire to see me suffer without you, Astrid."

"Your misery is certainly a selling point for me, sure, but that's not why. Just trust me on this. It'll make her life. And my job now is to make her happy."

Pierre thought for almost a minute about how to respond, the noose still around his neck. "And then you will owe me a favor that I can cash in when I please?"

"I don't think so. But I'll take it under advisement. And you should ask her really nicely, too. Something big, flamboyant, and European, like you're good at."

Pierre nodded with his eyes closed. "I will. For you." Then he gazed at me in an effort to force me to gaze back. "Astrid, you know, all I have for you is love. You are always too busy thinking about yourself to see that. Open your eyes, Astrid, and you will see what I see. I love you."

I still believe that Pierre didn't love me. Pierre loved writing poems about me. My name probably rhymes with a lot of words in whatever language he speaks. But whatever he felt for me was nothing. "Were you even listening to me?" he asked then.

"Maybe. Or maybe I was looking at my reflection in your napkin holder." I looked away from the napkin holder, which was at a really good angle for me. "Would you like me to show you how to tie that noose correctly?"

>>>>>>>>>>>>>

"It's seven o'clock," Dean Rein said.

"Fantastic," I replied. "And to think, just yesterday at this time it was also seven o'clock. What a roller coaster life is."

"Our appointment was for six."

"I had to go to Pierre's."

"Really?" he asked, raising his eyebrow. "A relationship is a good step for you."

"Ew. No. It was just one of his cries for help, but the noose broke the ceiling fan and he hurt his knees."

"My god, Astrid." He shook his head. "Everyone deserves help."

"Not Pierre. Talking to Pierre is like talking to a cloud. He's just gas and rain."

Dean Rein walked to a coffee machine and refilled a mug that had a cartoon of a dog on a therapist's couch, telling his problems to another dog. "Have you added anything to your list this week?"

I handed him a crumpled piece of paper. "Yup."

Dean Rein squinted a few times, as if he expected the words to change. "You bought hamburgers, Astrid?"

"A lot of hamburgers."

He took a pen and crossed it out. "Spending money doesn't require from you the same effort it does from others. You don't value money like the rest of the world."

"Everyone values money, sir. The more you have, the more you understand how much it can give you."

"I don't buy your logic, Astrid." That was fair. I was making it up as I went along. But by the end of it, I was convinced I was right. Dean Rein leaned in conspiratorially. "Why did you go see Pierre? You don't like him. You just said that."

"The same reason I ever see Pierre. Sometimes, and it surprises even me, he can be useful." I lowered my voice. "I have a plan."

Dean Rein shook his head and leaned back. "I'm familiar with many of your plans. It's the only reason I have the cell phone numbers for several agents at the Bureau of Alcohol, Tobacco, and Firearms."

"No, this is a plan for doing good stuff. I give you my word."

"Oh." He chuckled in the irritating way he always did. "Your word. To be frank, your word is about as valuable as a box of gossamer and dreams."

"How can your wife stand you?" I asked.

"She stands me just fine."

"Really? Why does she spend so much of the year without you in Vancouver?"

"She . . . Why do you know that?"

"Why wouldn't I know that? My plan is going to be good. So good, in fact, that by this time next week I'm going to be back at school here."

"You're aware that's not your decision."

"You'll let me back. And when I'm here, I want my room back."

"You can't have it back. It's somebody else's room now."

"I know it's someone else's room. But I want it."

"If you return to our school—and that's a big 'if'—you are entitled to a dorm room with a roommate. Like everybody else."

I thought over the option on the table. "If I agree to that, what are you going to give me?"

Dean Rein crinkled up his face like a deflated balloon, and then he laughed silently. He said, "You actually don't hold any cards here. Even humoring you is more than I owe you."

"So why are you even going through the motions, sir?"

He thought about it for a moment. "I don't know, Astrid. Maybe there's a part of me that's rooting for you."

>>>>>>>>>>>>

Two towns over, there was a giant mall called Griswold Square. It was the only mall in the county, so when people told me they were going to the mall, that's where they meant. Also, when people told me they were going to the mall, I would say, "AHHHHHH! Who cares? Why are you telling me this?"

There was an ice cream stand at the mall called "Cream 'n' Good," which managed not to make any sense and sound totally disgusting at the same time. That's where Mason worked. His uniform was a paper hat and a Hawaiian shirt.

"Do you remember me?" I asked him. "I am the girl who didn't pepper spray you in the face."

"A lot of girls didn't pepper spray me in the face. Like, all of them," he said.

"I can change that right now, if you'd like."

He looked uncertain of whether I was kidding. "Can I get you something?" he finally offered.

"Firstly, I'd like a cookie dough Typhoon, extra walnuts. Secondly, I need to talk business."

"Let me get your Typhoon first." Mason looked very different in his place of work. At school he looked like the sort of person who had dozens of pet snakes. But at the mall he looked like someone who maybe had only one snake. He mostly just looked like a kid who worked at an ice cream shop. It really drove home how much effort it takes for people to look scary. If they stopped working at it, it didn't keep up.

He handed me my Typhoon—vanilla ice cream, cookie dough, peanut butter cups, three kinds of sprinkles, Rice Krispies, whipped cream, extra walnuts, and two maraschino cherries. It was lovely. "I have to say this because I'll get in trouble with my manager if I don't," he said. "So: have a cream-filled day." He cleared his throat, perhaps trying to restore his dignity. "What's your business?" he asked when he was finished.

"Homecoming dance," I said. "Are you going?"

"No."

"I need you to go. And not with me."

"Dances are stupid. For stupid people. Who are stupid. You couldn't pay me to go. You don't have enough money."

"You work at an ice cream stand that charges by the gummi bear, and I'm very rich," I told him. "Of course I have enough money."

"It doesn't matter."

"Are you sure I can't entice you with a warehouse of

ugly shirts or really good tickets to an angry concert?"

"You act like you know me. You don't know anything about me."

"Again, I'm very rich. My grandfather has private investigators on retainer and the Internet is a giant pit of information. I know you work here. I know you got a scholarship to the Art Institute of Chicago but you're not sure if you should go because you think your band might take off. It won't. I know you got your heart broken last year by a girl named Tabitha and you don't have a good place to express your anger. And I know your brother spent two weeks in rehab and now he's very religious, your dad is in the navy, you lived in the Philippines for four years, and also, *puntang ina mo*.

"Did you just insult my mother in Tagalog?"

"Yeah, I only know how to curse in Tagalog. And you know what else I know—you owe me."

"Why do I owe you?" he said.

"You owe me because when I could've made you cry, I didn't. And that's something you'll appreciate when you think back on your high school days."

"I'll give you a free Typhoon. But that's it," he said.

"You'll go," I said.

"No."

"You will. Because something is going to happen there

that's pertinent to your interests and your life. If you miss it, well, you will have missed it forever."

Then I handed him a fifty-dollar bill and walked away.

>>>>>>>>>>>>

*By the way, Lucy wanted to be a "veterinarian's assistant" one day.

>>>>>>>>>>>>

### THINGS THAT EVERYONE SHOULD KNOW
### By Astrid Krieger

**Punching. (Make sure your thumb is outside your fist or you will break it.)**

**Basic lock picking. (You should also know complicated lock picking, but basic is enough for the short term.)**

**Essential bits of information about things boys like, in case you need something from them. These include but are not limited to football, Superman, and how to wear a baseball hat.**

**Where the nearest knives are located.**

**How to curse in at least three languages.**

Basic anatomy, i.e., where to hit or kick someone so it will hurt most.

How to make an Old Fashioned. (You might only need to know this if you and I have the same grandfather and he told you a hundred times that the only thing you really need to know in life is how to make an Old Fashioned. Either way, it's one sugar cube, three dashes of Angostura bitters, club soda, and a two-count of rye whiskey.)

# CHAPTER 16

# JIMMY RAINCOAT

Lisbet had been conspiring to dress me and do my hair and makeup for practically my whole life. I didn't know what the appeal of it was, but I didn't know a lot of things, like how microwave ovens worked. She was last able to fulfill her wish when I was about two years old, and she managed to get her hands on me just long enough to transform my toddler self into a horror movie clown-demon. Since then, I'd always managed to outrun her and her lipstick weapons. She would plead, "Please. I just want to flat iron your hair for two hours." Doing makeovers was not something Lisbet *wanted* to do. It was something she needed to do, similar to breathing and eating a celery stalk every other day.

But my streak of good luck was not going to last forever. This was her wedding day. She had a team of serious women waiting in the east wing of the house to powder her face and shine and lacquer her hair into a stiff architectural structure. On that day, she could have whatever she wanted, and she wanted to make me over. So I'd agreed. And it wasn't a trick. It happened.

After pulling hair extensions and sharp-heeled shoes from her closet, after holding the bridesmaid dress up to my body, and thinking, and going back into her closet, and thinking some more, and discovering a bra that "will be invisible to everyone," and after a long jag where she seemed to be building another person out of the air with her fingers—Lisbet tied me into a bunch of fabric. It had a lot of detailing that she referred to by a lot of names, but I can only describe it as a shiny yellow dress.

"You look so beautiful, Astrid," she said.

I was less immediately inclined to agree. "This dress makes me look like a Polish prostitute," I told her.

"Hey!" Lisbet had a lot of loyalty to clothes, and she did not like people speaking ill of them.

"And not like one of those Hungarian prostitutes with their *standards*."

"This dress was very expensive."

"Really? How much did you spend on this thing?"

Lisbet tried to do math, then gave up. "I don't know. I had it made in Tokyo, and I can't convert money in my head. But it was one point five million yen." Lisbet had me tilt my head up so she could administer powder to my cheeks, and she tilted her head down because I'd hurt her feelings.

"It's a very nice dress, Lisbet," I said. "You know how I am. This is just weird for me."

"I know. But it's great."

We were both quiet for a few minutes while Lisbet decorated my mouth. When she finished, I looked at myself in the mirror. As difficult as it was to admit, Lisbet had done a very nice job.

"Thank you," I said. "Thank you for making me look nice, Lisbet."

Lisbet smiled. "You're welcome."

"I'm sorry I put a dead frog in your flute when we were kids."

"You did?" she said. "It's okay. Everything is okay. Because at two o'clock, I'll be married."

Behind Lisbet was a stack of robin's-egg-blue boxes full of engagement presents she was planning on returning. All of a sudden, I realized they could be incredibly useful. "Can I have some of those?" I asked. "They'll go to a good cause. Every door is a window." Happily, she agreed.

The wedding planner instructed me to wait in the foyer until she gave the sign for the music to start and the walk down the aisle to proceed. The wait was long and boring. There had been a rehearsal dinner the night before, but no one had actually rehearsed anything. I had no idea what I was supposed to do when the event began. I had agreed to read a passage from Corinthians and anticipated it would be followed by a lightning strike and the wedding party getting swallowed up into the gates of hell. I had looked up my duties, and mostly I was just supposed to walk up the aisle and stand there, which was something I could definitely do. Also, I had yet to decide if, when the minister said, "*If anyone sees any reason why these two shouldn't be married blah blah forever hold your peace,*" I would say, "Fifty percent of marriages end in divorce," or "Lisbet farted." Both sounded good.

I was to walk down the aisle with the best man, Randy's friend from college, who said, "Everyone calls me Jimmy Raincoat. Wanna know why?"

"No," I said. "I don't wanna know why."

My dad and Vivi were also waiting in the foyer. Vivi smiled as if to say, "*This is the sort of daughter I signed up for. I signed up for a daughter who looks like this.*"

"You look beautiful, sweetie," my mother said. It may have been the first time she had ever said anything like that without adding something like, *But why must you make that face all the time?*

My father was puzzled. "Who does she look like?"

"I don't know," Vivi said.

"You don't know who I'm thinking of?"

"I don't."

Then my dad snapped his fingers, having figured it all out. "Leslie Van Houten."

"The Manson girl?" Vivi said.

"The prettiest Manson girl," he clarified. Leslie Van Houten murdered people in the sixties, but she also did happen to have nice cheekbones, so my father meant that as a compliment.

I felt a tap on my shoulder. It was Noah. His suit didn't fit him very well. He was holding a corsage. The box was all fogged up from being in the refrigerator all day. I was familiar with the look that boys get when they want to touch you or grab you or kiss you. He didn't look like that, though. It was more a look of admiration. Maybe it was the way you would look at the Grand Canyon from very far away. I certainly wasn't used to someone looking at me like that. I had no idea what to do with it.

"I was waiting in one of the big rooms, but I wanted to see you," he said. "You look beautiful."

"*Go on . . .*" I said, batting my eyelashes.

Noah took the corsage out of the box. It was white, purple, and yellow. He had done a good job finding flowers that looked nice with the dress. I thanked him and said, "How did you know I like presents?"

He left to sit down and wait for the processional with the other guests, but he returned five minutes later. He leaned in, a serious expression on his face, and whispered, "I heard something. I heard someone talking. I thought you needed to know."

"What?"

"I heard they, um, lost the groom."

"He's dead?" I asked.

"No," he said, "not that kind of 'lost.'"

The wedding planner was a stern woman named Ms. Antoinette, and she buzzed throughout the back hall and frowned and snapped her fingers a lot. I stopped her as she tried to whiz by me. I leaned in very close to her face. "Is there a problem?" I asked pointedly.

"Just stay here," she said. "It'll start soon."

"Listen, we could go back and forth like this or you can tell me. If you haven't noticed, I'm the maid of god-damn honor."

"We can't find the groom," she whispered, looking nervously toward the crowd of restless guests.

"And you've looked everywhere? Couch cushions? Are

you sure you're not confusing him for one of the caterers? He's very uninteresting looking."

She shook her head.

"Does my sister know?"

Ms. Antoinette shook her head again. "No. Not yet."

"Don't say anything. How long can you stall?"

"However long I have to," she said.

I grabbed my cousin Gretchen by the arm. "You stay with this woman, okay?" I told Gretchen. "Make sure Lisbet is happy. And that she stays happy. Sing to her or something. Keep her distracted."

"Well, hello to you too, Astrid," Gretchen said.

"I have no time for this."

"The last time I saw you, you closed a piano lid on my nose."

"It won't happen again. I promise. I don't even know where the piano is anymore."

I casually walked over to the best man. I didn't want to make a scene or anything. I said, "Listen, I need you to tell me—"

"Why they call me Jimmy Raincoat? Of course," he said. "Back in college, it rained for all of October and at the same time my roommate's name actually *was* Jimmy—"

"Forget it," I said and took Noah by the arm. "Let's find my grandfather."

>>>>>>>>>>>>>

My grandfather was in his library, which I found odd, because he should've been outside waiting for the wedding to start like everyone else. I figured it was because he was very old and tended to forget a lot of things. (He referred to Lisbet as "Wanda" at least five times a day.) But this was still weird. Most of the guests were people he knew, and my grandfather liked seeing me in nice clothes.

"Stay here," I said to Noah. "Don't say anything to him, okay?"

Noah nodded.

"There's a wedding going on, you know?" I said to my grandfather.

"Is there a groom?" he wanted to know.

"How did you know there wasn't?"

"Does it matter? It means I can stay here all I want, can't I? No groom, no wedding."

"Where is he?"

"Wanda will meet someone else, I'm sure. She has a real fertile look. Let's get out of here. I have at least three children of mine on the main lawn, and I'd like to duck away before your uncle Ellery starts asking for money."

"We need a groom. I need to do this for Lisbet. Please. Tell me what you know."

"I need to go to a bar," he said.

"I'll make you a drink right here."

"No. The groom. I left him in a bar. If you want him, I'm sure he's still there."

I didn't know what to say, but I didn't have time to fight about it.

"How are you, son?" Grandpa had finally noticed Noah.

"This is Noah," I said.

My grandfather waved the smoke around the room. "Don't you think I know who Noah is?" There was no reason my grandfather should have known who Noah was.

"No, Grandpa," I said. "The Noah you're thinking of is the one with the ark." Then I looked back at Noah. "Grandpa and Noah with the ark went to high school together."

"You know how to drive, kid?" my grandfather said.

"Yes," Noah replied.

"Fine. We'll save the wedding, then. Unless you can think of a more entertaining way to spend our afternoon. I can think of thousands."

>>>>>>>>>>>>>

"Not this one," the senator said. We had been to three bars in Cadorette. Noah drove like he was carpooling a soccer team of seven-year-olds, so we'd already wasted an absurd amount of time. "It's the one where they don't show sports. There's no television at the bar I'm thinking of."

"With all due respect, sir, I just need to know the name of the place," Noah said.

"Do you really think I'd go to a bar where the ladies are dressed as referees? I require my liquor from a man in shirtsleeves. It would be a mistake to trust anyone else," Grandpa said.

"He likes the hotel bar," I said, remembering where it was.

I looked at my grandfather as we drove. He was slipping. Everyone knew he was slipping. But I'd never really believed it. My whole life, he always knew what he was doing. Even on days when he forgot to put on pants, he'd had his reasons. It was just that lately, he must've had a lot of reasons for not putting on pants. Finally I saw the hotel coming up on the right, and I told Noah to pull over.

"Are you going to give me any information or am I

paddling alone here?" I asked my grandfather. "Why isn't Lisbet's fiancé at his wedding?"

"He made a choice," my grandfather said. "I'm the kind of man who gives people choices. But I can't make up his mind for him."

"Very helpful," I said as I stepped out of the car.

"What did you bring? What are you going to do to him?" Grandpa said. "Is there a knife in the glove compartment I don't know about? Remember what I taught you about sea anemones."

"I didn't bring anything," I said. "I'm not going to hurt him. I'm just going to make this better."

Grandpa laughed. "Sure thing, kitten."

I looked at Noah, who was giving me a pleading look.

"No matter what he says, don't cry around my grandfather," I instructed him.

"Don't worry," Grandpa said. "We'll have a nice talk too."

# CHAPTER 17

# YOU WERE WITH ME AND I WAS WITH YOU

It wasn't my first time in a bar. My father and my grand-father sometimes had to stop in places like this all around the world for business, so when I went along, I would usually sit in a booth and carve things into the table or bet drunks twenty dollars that they couldn't drink a glass of black pepper, Tabasco sauce, and dishwater. Even if they won, they lost, and those were the best kinds of bets. It wasn't even my first time in that particular bar, but in the daylight it looked sadder than I remembered.

It wasn't hard to miss Randy, despite the fact that it was almost always incredibly easy to miss Randy. That day he was the only one there. If there had been maybe two other people with brown hair in the bar, I might have had to replace Randy with someone else and hope that Lisbet wouldn't be able to tell the difference. A similar plan had once worked with a goldfish that I'd accidentally dropped in the toaster, so I thought it was likely to work again.

"Can I see some ID, miss?" the bartender said. I handed him a fake passport, and he nodded. "That's quite a dress for a Saturday afternoon, Miss Graneveis."

"If you're not going to go out with style, why the hell go out?" I said.

"What can I get you?"

"She'll have some sort of red sweet juice if you have anything like that," Randy said. It was the first time I'd ever heard him say anything.

"How did you know what I drink?"

"How wouldn't I? We live in the same house," he said.

I felt a little bad just then that I hadn't paid as much attention to what Randy drinks. "How long have you been here?" I asked Randy.

"He's been here too goddamn long," the bartender said.

"Your grandfather said I can stay here as long as I want, so I have a feeling I'm just going to stay here all night and right through the wedding tomorrow, if I feel like it."

"Today is tomorrow," I said. "Your wedding is now."

"What is in this drink?" he asked, looking down at his hands as if he now had four instead of two.

I motioned to the bartender. "Get him some coffee or something, barkeep. Is it cool to call you 'barkeep'?"

He nodded that it was cool and poured Randy a coffee. "Did he say something to you? My grandfather?" I asked Randy. "Did he threaten you?"

"He's been great," Randy said. "He told me that he knows I have dreams, and he doesn't think anyone should stop me from realizing those dreams."

"What are your dreams?" I asked, hating myself even as I uttered it. Frankly, I don't even remember what he said. Something about competitive crossword puzzles, soap sculpture, moth collecting, bread making, sports medicine, or maybe animal husbandry. Or it was something else? Who cares?

"What does that have to do with anything?" I asked when he was finished. "Go for it. Live the dream. Husband some animals. You have forever."

"I don't have forever. After I get married, I'll work for your family's company. And then I'll become just another cog in the machine. It's very sad."

"That is a little sad. And what did my grandfather have to say about that?"

"He said I didn't have to work there and that I didn't have to get married at all. He said that he would write me a check so I wouldn't marry Lisbet."

I felt a weird tightness in my chest. And I had a vivid picture in my head of the senator with an unlit cigar laughing at his incredible plan. But I didn't understand it. My whole life, my grandfather and I had understood each other completely. It was almost like we shared a brain, except that my brain had slightly more knowledge about how a computer worked and his had a little more information about fifty-year-old scotch and Lana Turner movies. But I couldn't figure out why he would try to pay Randy to make Lisbet sad. And it made me angry. Not at Randy, but at my grandfather.

"How much money did he offer you?"

"*Lots*," he said.

"So do you want to marry her or not?"

"I don't know," Randy said. "I'm not sure." Then he started to cry. It wasn't a dignified, manly, military-funeral cry. It was like a six-year-old girl who'd gotten scratched by a kitten. And then it got worse. Randy put his head on my shoulder and moaned into the ruffles of my dress. By then, I'd had enough. I put the palm of my hand on his forehead and lifted it up.

I don't think Dean Rein would have been very impressed by how I dealt with Randy. He probably would've encouraged me to slowly stroke his hair as he cried on my shoulder. But even in the very kindest part of my being, that wasn't going to happen. What I thought about was my sister, and how if this day didn't end the way she wanted it to end, she wasn't going to be happy. Lisbet wanted this wedding, and she wanted it to be with Randy. I didn't have to understand it. I just had to make sure it happened.

So I said, "Listen, I need to make you aware of something. I don't care about you. I don't care whether you live or die. All I know is that my sister wants to marry you. And if my sister is not married in thirty minutes, you'd better not be interested in having working knees. Are we clear, buddy?"

He sniffed a little. "How do you know what your sister wants? We barely ever see you."

"I'm . . . I'm working on that."

"She's not always happy, you know. She gets sad a lot. It's not a very happy house over there."

"I . . . I know it's not happy over there. Lisbet is unhappy too? Is anybody happy?"

"I don't know." Randy wasn't looking to run away because he wanted a big check. He just didn't know how to make Lisbet happy for the rest of her life. I had always figured it would take nothing more than a school bus and a box of rainbow sprinkles to make Lisbet happy forever. But maybe I was not the only person in the world who was more complicated than everyone assumed.

"Do you love her?" I asked.

"Sure," Randy said.

"Sure? Or yes?"

"Yes. I love her very much. I just don't know if now is the right—"

"Get in the goddamn car," I said. "Because girls tend to have a hard time staying in love with guys who stand them up on their wedding day."

He looked at me desperately.

"I'm serious."

"I'm sorry. About all this. The wedding. Lisbet . . ." he whispered. "I really do want to make her happy."

"Perfect," I said. "Then get in the car."

>>>>>>>>>>>>

My father cried as he watched Lisbet get married. He said to me, "It's times like these when I say to myself, look at these two girls. You and Lisbet. Look at you. I made you. And then you two, you grew up. I guess that's what it's all about. You make people, and they grow up. It's the meaning of life. It's very sad."

Lisbet never knew that she almost didn't get married. Gretchen distracted her for almost an hour by retying the back of her dress several times and weighing her advice over what kind of bow was the best kind of bow. Then Gretchen, Ms. Antoinette, and Lisbet sang three songs from *The Sound of Music*, and Lisbet lost complete sense of time. Even though I'm writing this down right here, I doubt Lisbet's ever going to read this book and thus she will never know. This book contains no pictures of cute puppies or Junior Jumbles, so it's probably not pertinent to her interests. That's perfectly fine with me. She smiled the whole wedding, and a lot of people took pictures of her, and I know that's the sort of thing that will always be important to Lisbet. When it was time for Lisbet to say *I do*, she said, "I do. I really, really very much do."

I could tell my grandfather was avoiding me for most of the ceremony. He couldn't get around easily anymore, but amazingly he found a way to wheel to whatever place I was not at all times. I asked Noah what they talked about while I was in the bar, and Noah said, "Nothing really. Mostly about Lyndon Johnson's favorite gentlemen's clubs." This sounded fairly accurate, though I could tell there was more. Noah just said, "Nope. That's it." He was a terrible liar. His hands got sweaty when he lied. Or maybe his hands were always sweaty. Or maybe he was always lying.

At eight o'clock, I suggested we leave for the homecoming dance. Most of the really important people had left the wedding (though the secretary of defense was still passed out in the greenhouse). Also, Lisbet's beautiful bridesmaid dress kept poking me in the belly button.

When we got to the end of the driveway where Noah was parked, the senator was there waiting.

"Goodbye," I said.

He took a long swig from a flask. In it was either bourbon or Pepto-Bismol. He had flasks for both. "You're off?" he wanted to know.

"Yeah."

"In this car, huh?"

"It would appear that way."

He took another drink. "I didn't really want to have kids," he said. "I tried to parent Dirk and Ellery and Martinique. But my heart wasn't really in it, you know."

I wasn't sure what he was talking about, but I said, "Yes, I know," because I could tell that wasn't the important part of whatever he was trying to say.

"But I really tried hard with you," he continued. "Do you remember your alibis?"

I nodded. He was of course referencing how, when I was six years old, he'd told me that I always needed to have a list of alibis handy in case shit ever went down. And—as he pointed out—shit was always going to go down.

"Let me hear them," he said.

I glanced at Noah. We had to leave, but Noah looked more like he needed to leave the state than he needed to get to the homecoming dance, so I figured we could linger a minute longer. "Okay, fine. First is I was kidnapped by a sex addict. Then, I have an identical twin. Then, I got locked in the car trunk. Also . . . I'm retarded, and I don't know where I am."

"Right."

"And you were with me and I was with you. That's all I remember," I said.

"There were six."

"But that's all I remember."

"That's too bad," he said. "You're missing the most important." He paused for effect. "The world turned and flung me."

At age six, I had learned that nobody was ever actually standing still. The world was spinning really, really fast. It seemed perfectly reasonable to me that one day it would slow down a little or speed up, and you might be thrown a few miles and end up in a place you'd never expected to be. It seemed likely. *Sorry, officer, I understand that I was apprehended in that bank vault, but it wasn't my fault. The world turned and flung me.*

"Do you know why I tried so hard with you?" my grandfather asked.

"Because you think I'm like you," I replied.

"Yeah. That's why you were my favorite. Because you were like me. That's what I thought."

I didn't know if I was supposed to say thank you or leave or what. I said nothing.

"I was wrong," he said. "You're not like me at all." He looked beyond me, focusing on some distant point.

"You're drunk," I told him.

"I'm disappointed," he said.

"In me?"

"Remember when I said that there are three things you'll be wrong about when you get old?"

"Yeah." I waited to hear more.

"Well, I know mine now." I didn't ask him what they were, but I should have. Because he chose that moment to turn his wheelchair around and wheel away. I didn't know it at the time, but I would never be able to ask him again.

"Bye, Astrid," he called out behind him. "Have fun."

## LETTER FROM MONTGOMERY KRIEGER
## (DATED TWO MONTHS PRIOR)

**Dear Monkey,**

**It's your grandpa writing to you. I know you probably don't believe it because this letter is typed on a stupid computer, but my hands have been too**

damn stiff lately, so that idiot Barry who works for me is going to write down everything I say. And he'd better have written down that he's an idiot when I called him an idiot just now or else he's going to have to look for a new job as soon as he can get his butt out the door. I just checked to make sure he wrote it down, and he did, and that's good.

I'm writing to you today because I told you I would, and you will never get me to write a god-damn email like you asked. A good letter should take two days at least to get to the person or else why don't you just go to them and tell them whatever it is you want to say, right? I've been thinking about you lately for a lot of reasons. Chiefly, it's because I'm sitting here on my butt all the livelong day, and I have nothing to do but think. I'm half blind, so I can't tell the difference between a book and a sand-box at this point, and thinking is the only thing I can do that doesn't require me to move. But the reason I'm thinking about you in particular is because I know that this is your last year at Bristol.

Maybe you don't think that matters, but my last year at Bristol was damn important to me. There were a bunch of reasons for that: it was right on the precipice of the war, as you know, and that year was the last year when all of us boys were able to be carefree and alive. Half my buddies would be strewn across Iwo Jima in pieces just a few years later. I say "all of us boys," because there weren't any ladies at Bristol back then. Men only. If we wanted to see ladies, we'd have to go fifteen miles to the Chester School for Girls when they had dances. That's when I met your first grandmother.

She wasn't your actual grandmother. Not the one who had your father. But she was my first wife (my marriage to Jean Harlow was not legal in every sense of the word, so she doesn't count). I was seventeen, and I could barely shave, but I still knew when a moment was important. Her name was Agnes. She, too, left this world during the war, when her flight to Osaka was shot down (she was working for the other side, but I didn't know it at the time).

This is the last year before your life happens in ways you don't always want it to. It's your last Bristol bonfire. It's your last Bristol dance marathon. It's your last Bristol lacrosse game. I know you don't do any of those things because they're stupid, but they're still the last ones. My point is, it was around that time (during my last year) that I made a decision for myself—a decision I am pretty sure you have made for yourself. The decision was this: don't let yourself be the sort of person whose plane gets shot down over Osaka. If you're going to go out, go out the way you want. Always.

I will leave you now because I got to sleep. It's two in the afternoon. Don't ever get old.

Love,
M

# CHAPTER 18

# ASTRID KRIEGER IS SUCH A BITCH

The theme of the homecoming dance was Monte Carlo, but if the attempt was to make the cafeteria look like Monte Carlo, it was a colossal failure. To be fair, I was probably the only person at the homecoming dance who'd actually been to Monte Carlo, so the lack of attention to detail was forgivable. And really, who would decorate a dance with images of hairy-chested Formula 1 drivers trying to lick your face and take you to their yachts?

A roll of red crepe paper had been rolled down the wheelchair ramp to give the feel of a fancy red carpet. Clumps of tangled Christmas lights were strewn randomly over bleachers. One sad bowl of pretzels shaped like suits of cards was positioned in the center of an otherwise empty table. A photographer took pictures of people with their dates and also of a few unhappy kids standing alone in front of what looked like aluminum foil. There was a DJ. The DJ had a banner hanging from the table suggesting that he was New York City's top party DJ, but it was clear that he had graduated from Cadorette a few years back and still lived in town with his parents. In between songs, he pointed out more than once that Ms. Savarirayan, who taught chemistry, was "still lookin' foxy."

I was overdressed in my gown. Most of the girls wore dresses that showed off their stomachs. One sophomore was about five months pregnant, so her dress provided easy access in case somebody had to perform an emergency C-section. Noah was also overdressed in his suit. Most of the boys wore dress shirts that belonged to their fathers and little else to suggest that they were actually dressing up. At least three kids wore khaki cargo shorts. Like they'd rushed away from exploring the jungle and didn't have time to throw on some pants. I felt a little bad for some of the girls at the dance. Even the girls I didn't like deserved a date who was wearing pants.

I kind of liked dancing. I hadn't danced at all at Lisbet's wedding because I didn't want to be groped by any congresspeople. But I danced with no problems at the homecoming dance. I didn't know much about the songs they were playing, but they were fast. Noah and I and Lucy and Pierre danced in the center of the room until I was pretty much out of breath.

Pierre, unsurprisingly, was a great dancer. He had been

a ballerina since he was, like, three. I'd told him on several occasions that (a) maybe it wasn't something to brag about and (b) I didn't think they called male ballet dancers ballerinas, but he didn't care.

Much to the surprise of the entire world, Lucy was also a pretty good dancer. She was graceful and flexible. It almost made me reevaluate the ways I thought about everyone. It was possible that I wasn't scratching the surface of what people were good at. It was certainly a lesson I should've learned from Talia Pasteur. Talia wasn't just good at being a tree. She was also pretty good at getting me kicked out of Bristol. And that lesson could be applied to almost anyone. Maybe Dean Rein was a brilliant flamenco guitarist.

"I'm going to take a break," I said to Noah when the song ended. "You stay out here, okay?"

He nodded and continued with his "dancing," or maybe he was having an epileptic seizure. I sat down and looked out across the cafeteria. I wondered for a minute about where I would be at that same moment if I hadn't been forced to leave Bristol. I certainly wouldn't have been wearing a giant gown. It was a Saturday night, so I would've probably been in my dorm room. Or maybe I would've been in jail. I wondered if I could've gotten my usual private cell or if I would've had to share. I wondered about this girl I shared a cell with once. Her name was

Sandy. I wondered if she'd killed her boyfriend yet.

Pierre sat next to me. "This is nice, you think?" he said.

"I kind of do," I said. And I kind of did.

"Have you tried the punch? It's better than I could have imagined. I think someone spiked it with Everclear."

I stood up. "I'm going to step out."

Pierre put his hand on my shoulder, coating it with a gross layer of sweat. "Would you like me to come with you?"

I grabbed his wrist, twisting it fast and hard. "No," I said.

He said, "Ow. Ow. Ow. Ow. My wrist."

I pointed to the floor and told him to keep dancing. The evening had been going almost perfectly according to plan. Everyone was around who was supposed to be around. Everything that was happening was supposed to happen. I felt pretty good about myself at that moment. Everything that went wrong did so much later that night.

I left the cafeteria and made for the bathroom.

In the bathroom, there was a mass of voices blaring like train whistles as a group of girls reapplied eye makeup in the mirror in giant, goopy strokes.

"I hate that girl. She gives me a feeling I just hate."

"Yeah, I know, I get it. She's rich. But why is she even here? If she's so rich, why doesn't she buy somewhere else? And then go there."

"Yeah. Like, she should buy like another country. Far, far away. Bye. See you later. Hope you never come back."

"Did you hear about what she did with the burgers?"

"Yeah."

"I don't need your burgers. I don't need you to, like, buy me dinner. I already ate dinner."

"You should look at it this way, right? I mean, she thinks she's all hot and she thinks she's so great and everything, but then that's who she brings to the dance. I was, like, laughing. I was literally laughing. So much. I literally died when I saw her with him."

"Yeah. And nice dress. It's the homecoming dance, not . . . the queen of England's house."

"Right."

"I know. Right?"

"Astrid Krieger."

"Yeah, that girl sucks."

"I know."

"I know."

"Astrid Krieger is a bitch. Astrid Krieger is such a bitch."

I had been sitting in a bathroom stall, just taking a break, for almost ten minutes. I had known this was the sort of thing I would eventually hear. I had heard of how girls spent most of their time in the bathroom talking about girls they hated, but I had never experienced it until I came to Cadorette. It's supposedly a phenomenon that happens with girls everywhere, but I'd never used a public restroom before going to school at Cadorette. When girls were saying mean things about other girls at Bristol, it was usually whispered in the dining hall or shouted across an open lawn.

I knew that girls I was barely aware of hated me. That had been true everywhere for my whole life. You would think it would bother me more, but it really didn't. Heavy hangs the head that wears the crown, I suppose. I had known that they would talk about me. And I didn't care. But I needed them to know I was there, so I flushed the toilet and walked out of the stall.

The girls whom I had been eavesdropping on were Summer Wonder and her friends: the skinny girl with the slumped shoulders and the other one with the freckles and the hair.

Summer Wonder tried to look like she'd expected me to be behind her, but I could tell she hadn't. She was at least a little bit scared, but she didn't want her friends to know. "You don't put your feet down when you pee?" she asked.

"There's so much about how I pee that you'll never understand," I said.

Then Summer Wonder said, "Are you going to cry now?" and she said it in a way that was mock crying so that, if I was going to start crying, I would know how it was done.

"No. Why would I do that?"

Slumpy Shoulders said, "Because we—"

"Because you said stuff about me. I would say that you were ninety percent accurate. Let me think. Nothing that wasn't true, for the most part. I do think I'm so great. I am so rich. I did bring that spaz to the dance. And I am a bitch. I totally am."

The looks they gave me were strange. I don't think anyone expects you to agree with them when they insult you. It totally knocks them off balance, though. I would recommend it in almost all situations where you might be insulted. Because what could they possibly say back? You just agreed with them.

Freckles said something like, "What's wrong with you?"

I ignored her. "I'll take issue with one point. I don't suck. At least, I don't think so. But that might just be because I think I'm so great. And that's a point where we all agree."

Summer Wonder said, "Awesome. We all agree. Now leave."

"I would," I said. "But I need something from you skankholes."

"Who the—?"

"Fine. We'll agree to disagree on whether or not you're skankholes," I said. "But this is what I need from you. When they announce homecoming king, you probably won't be happy. When they announce homecoming queen, you definitely won't be happy."

This made Summer Wonder laugh. Slumpy Shoulders and Freckles also laughed, probably because they felt they were supposed to.

"I'm going to be homecoming queen," Summer said.

"Summer is—" Slumpy said.

"Summer is not going to be homecoming queen. And it's not because you're kind of ugly and sort of cross-eyed. It's for a completely different reason. But when it's announced, I want you to cheer. Really loudly and without irony. And get other people to do it too."

"You think you're going to be homecoming queen?" Summer laughed, not because anything funny had been said, but because she wasn't being at all genuine.

"Because you're not," Slumpy Shoulders said.

"We made sure of that," Summer said.

"Good," I said. "I made sure of it too."

Then they were confused. They might have traded in a trip or seven to second base for some influence in these matters. It would turn out to be time poorly spent under their bras.

"You're not going to be happy," I said. "But I'm going to need your help. I still need you to cheer."

Summer tilted her head in my direction. "Why do you hate us?" she asked.

"I hate bullies."

Summer snorted. "But you're a bully. You mashed a Twinkie into my head."

"Nuh-uh," I said. "You're a bully. I'm a bully to bullies, and that is not a bully. That's a hero."

"Then why should we help you?" Summer said.

"Because," I said, "I've had a change of heart about jerks. Everyone always thought I was a jerk, even me, but I know now that deep down, I'm not a jerk. Maybe deep down, there are very few true horrible jerks. So you should help me because we are alike. And neither of us wants to be thought of as an asshole forever."

Summer thought about this. "Not a good enough reason."

"Fine," I said. "I also have presents." I opened the door to the bathroom stall where I'd been sitting. There was a large bag hanging on the purse hook. It was the kind of bag that Santa Claus would bring around for Christmas if Santa Claus traded toys for favors. From it, I took out a robin's-egg-blue box. "This is a necklace from Tiffany's. It's yours. And girls, if you want something from Tiffany's too, I got lots. And I mean lots."

They glanced at each other, then glanced back at the boxes. Their decision had been made.

"When it's time, you'll know."

>>>>>>>>>>>>

Kids smoked outside the fire doors at the end of C hall. That's where I figured I would find Mason during the dance.

I'd met bullies who were actual crazy people. There was a boy named Jacques Durang whose father was an international assassin. Jacques Durang was pretty much evil. When I was thirteen, I kicked him so hard he had to have testicle retrieval surgery. That was the first time anyone had ever asked me, "Do you know who my father is?" He said it as he was moaning on the ground. I did know who his father was, and I didn't care.

Mason wasn't a fully realized bully. I mean, Jacques Durang would've never sold ice cream at a mall. Mason was an aspiring bully, and that's why I figured he would be outside smoking with Melty. They must've thought smoking cigarettes fit the part. But they should have known that if they really wanted to effectively inflict pain on a victim, it would help if they didn't get winded while chasing someone up a staircase. Don't smoke because it makes it a lot harder to beat someone up. That's my public service message.

They put their cigarettes out quickly when I opened the door, and I could see the fear on their faces when they recognized me. "You," I said to Melty, making a shooing motion with my hand. "Go away." And he did. Fast.

"You're here," I said to Mason. "I'm glad you see things my way."

"Yeah, I'm here." Mason leaned against the wall. "What do you want with me? I have things to do."

"I don't think you have anything to do. And you know what, I also don't think you're a bad person," I said.

"I am a bad person," he said.

"No, you're not," I said. "You're an artist." In addition to the mural hanging in the cafeteria, he'd painted some of the decorations for the dance. They weren't really about Monte Carlo. They also weren't about homecoming. They were mostly about bats. But they were good. I wouldn't hang them in my rocket ship or anything, but I have specific tastes.

"I do some stuff," he said.

"I know. Redeemable. That's good. You're not just going to be doing me a favor, Mason. I'm also doing a favor for you."

"Don't do me any favors," he said.

"Nah. You'll like it."

"What is it?" he said.

"How would you like to fall in love tonight?"

# CHAPTER 19

# THE CORONATION

I stood in the back of the cafeteria and watched.

The DJ played something that sounded very royal, with a lot of horns. An empty circle opened up in the middle of the dance floor. Ben, the student council president, read down a long list of local businesses who sponsored the homecoming dance and then a bunch of announcements about some boring lit magazine fund-raiser, and maybe he went through step-by-step directions for how to bake a strawberry shortcake. I have no idea. I stopped listening. That guy was boring.

Then the music changed to a recording of a drumroll, and Principal Barth took the mic. He read the homecoming court and said something specific about each person. "She's a math something" and "He's a baseball something." Whatever. It was nice. They were freshmen and sophomores and juniors and who cares. I mean, some people cared—they had friends watching—but I was only there for the main event. I couldn't help but smile. I couldn't wait to see everyone's faces.

What happened was this: homecoming king was awarded to Mason. Nobody gasped at that, I'm pretty sure, but most people thought it was some sort of joke. Homecoming king was never as big a deal as queen. The student body regularly awarded the title to burnouts, cartoon characters, or people who had graduated eight years before.

The surprise was entirely because of the homecoming queen. Even I was a little surprised, and I had planned the whole thing. Principal Barth was surprised when he read it off his card, and I'm sure he was the one who wrote it down on the card in the first place.

The most surprised of all was Lucy Redlich. She wasn't even anywhere near that part of the floor. She was in the back with a handful of Cheez Doodles stuffed in one side of her mouth and a glob of hair in the other side. (Though I like to remember the moment without her having orange residue all over her face.) Principal Barth had to say her name three times before she could even figure out why her name was being amplified. But when she heard, her reaction was perfect. She didn't shake with nerves or run away, or slouch and shuffle her body to the front of the room. She smiled. She showed her teeth. She straightened her back, and she practically glided onto the stage.

I don't think Lucy could hear anything but the music in her head. I don't think she could see anything but what was right in front of her. She smiled, and it felt really good to see it. People talk about how it feels good to do good things, and they're right: it feels great. It's a little better than a lobster, though I've had better massages. But they never gave a masseuse the Nobel Peace Prize, so it's not just the feeling that's important.

Mason stood next to Lucy. He didn't smile in the same way she did when they crowned him homecoming king, but he seemed happy to be standing there. They blushed. They looked back and forth from the crowd to each other. Their fingers touched a little bit. It was kind of gross. But it also made sense. They were the number 1o.

I tapped Lucy on the shoulder and took a tiara from my bag. It was platinum and covered in rubies. "This once belonged to the princess of Austria," I said. "Don't let them put that plastic piece of crap on your head."

"I can't take your tiara," Lucy said.

"Of course you can. You're the queen."

The crowd wasn't as immediately taken by the moment. Some of them yelled and booed and someone screamed things like, "Your face is ugly," to Lucy, but that lasted only for a few seconds. Eventually you couldn't hear any boos at all.

I didn't understand Summer Wonder. I didn't know why people cared about what she thought about things or why they decided that her weird eyes were beautiful. But when she had an opinion about something, a lot of the school decided to have the same opinion. So, when Summer Wonder and her friends cheered and clapped for Lucy, the school lined up behind her. Summer Wonder probably really wanted to be up there instead, but she didn't want it nearly as much as she wanted Lisbet's jewelry. Everybody has a price.

A girl came up to me and said, "Summer said that you would give me something if I cheered."

"She did?" I said. I gave her a sterling silver baby rattle. I had no idea why Lisbet had been given one of those in the first place.

"How many people did you have to bribe to make this happen?" Noah wanted to know.

"Everyone but you."

"You solved all this with money."

"Nope. I solved *some* of this with money. But the real change happened with my people skills."

"What about all that Tiffany stuff?"

"I didn't buy that stuff. I took it. Big difference."

"Why didn't you try to bribe me?"

"What help were you going to provide?"

He thought about it. "I mean, you're never going to know until you bribe me."

"What would you like?" I asked.

He got this kind of sneaky smile. "Dance with me," he said.

I said, "I guess that would be okay."

They played a slow song.

I don't know what the song was. I remember that the song had a story, though it wasn't incredibly clear exactly what was going on and it was a little creepy. There was this girl. And she had a lot of dreams when she slept. And so she preferred to sleep instead of being awake and she slept whenever she could. But sometimes, she had to be awake (to eat and to go to work or whatever). And then she met a guy and fell in love immediately, which I found a little bit rash. And then instead of sleeping, she only wanted to see him even though she was tired pretty much all the time. And then she wondered if maybe she had actually been sleeping the whole time and her love wasn't real and what would happen if she woke up? And then they got in a car accident because she was so tired, and the guy died, and it proved that she wasn't sleeping. But the guy was still dead, so she slept more so she could dream about him.

"What are you thinking about?" Noah asked.

"Oh. Nothing, really. Logic problems with this song, mostly."

"You know, when your grandfather said before that he was disappointed, I don't think he meant—"

"I don't want to talk about it."

"It's just that—"

"No. Really. I don't."

"It's just that . . . he didn't mean it in a bad way."

"Noah, he and I . . . we mean everything in a bad way."

Noah smiled a little. "No, you don't. Not him either. When we were in the car together and you were in the hotel bar—he told me that you've turned out better than he could ever be."

"I'm not."

"You are. He believes it. I think so too." Noah stopped talking, and I could feel his hand on my back, and it wasn't a particularly bad feeling.

We sat down on the bleachers while Pierre was flirting

with Ms. Sharp. He was doing as bad a job with her as he did with everyone else in the world.

First, he asked her to dance.

Then she said it wouldn't be appropriate.

Pierre said, "Why? I won't be handsy if you don't want me to."

"You're a little young," Ms. Sharp said.

"Really? How old are you?"

"I'm twenty-three."

"Ah," Pierre said. "To be twenty-three again."

Pierre wasn't really winning her over. "What are you doing in high school, then?" Ms. Sharp wanted to know.

Pierre whispered, "I know where all the cocaine is."

He looked at me for some sort of approval, but I shook my head to let him know that he should give up.

>>>>>>>>>>>>

Lucy and Mason could have been anywhere else in the world. They didn't pay attention to anyone in the room. From where we sat, I could hear bits and pieces of their conversation. Mason asked Lucy if she liked the song that was playing, and Lucy said she didn't know because she was tone-deaf. Then Mason said he was color-blind and that's why he started wearing black. Then he realized it scared people, so he kept wearing black. Then Lucy asked Mason if he liked the song, and he said it sucked. But, also, that it was okay. Really romantic stuff, those two.

Lucy had said she wanted to be in love, and there they were, the two of them. Were they in love? Who knew. But they looked happy.

"They look happy," Noah said.

"Yeah," I said.

"You look happy too."

I had to laugh at that because, I don't know, I'd never thought of myself as a happy person. When I saw people like Lisbet walking around with their big goofy smiles all the time, I didn't think of that as a look I wanted for myself. I pretty much just saw that as the look someone had when they didn't realize they were about to get hit by a train.

On the other hand, I felt happy then, and it was nice. It was a little because of Lucy and Mason. It was also partly because of Noah. And then there was some part of me that just felt content in a way that I can't really explain.

Noah and I just sat there for song after song, until the dance was over. We just sat there until it was time to go, and then we left.

# CHAPTER 20

# A PIANO FALLING INTO THE OCEAN

The walk that Noah and I took from the front of the estate across the lawn and past the main house felt like hours and miles. It was probably only twenty minutes, but I was feeling a little dramatic, and twenty minutes still happens to be a long time to walk from the end of a driveway to a house in most situations. Noah and I had a lot to say on that journey. Here's some of the stuff I remember us talking about:

Noah used to do spelling bees when he was a kid. He was very competitive and, as he said, he did "very well." I told him it was actually impossible to do "very well" at a spelling bee because even if you won the thing, you were probably way worse off than if you'd never been involved in a spelling bee in the first place. He kind of agreed.

Noah said that the one thing he was more afraid of than anything else was mice. I laughed at him and said that mice don't do anything. He disagreed. He said that they carry a lot of disease. And I said that everything carries a lot of disease, and so what, you could use a disease or two.

So he asked me what I was afraid of, and I said nothing. And he said I was lying, and I said, "Well, I guess you'll never know."

Noah had had a girlfriend for a year. I was very surprised. I kept telling him how surprised I was. He said, "You're that surprised that I had a girlfriend before?" And I said, "I'm surprised that you've met a girl before." And he said, "You're kidding, right?" And I said, "Sure, right, whatever."

Her name was Julie and she was ugly. He never said that, but it's how I pictured her. I pictured her as ugly with a messed-up hand.

Noah has this website where he dresses his cat up as literary characters. This was also a reason that I was surprised he'd ever met a girl.

We then talked about how some gorillas know sign language. I am not positive how we got on the subject. It was an interesting thing, though.

Noah got quiet for a long time, and then he started saying a bunch of words that made no sense together, but I knew exactly what he was trying to say. If you spend any amount of time with a boy, you are bound to have a conversation pretty much exactly like that one. I'd managed to avoid getting too deeply involved in those sorts of things, but that's because I had always been pretty good at identifying exactly when it was happening. With Noah it began like this: "You know," he said. "You know how when two people, um, when they know each other. When a guy and a girl, they, um, they sometimes, they . . . You know, when . . . I've been. Here's the thing . . ."

That's people for you. They almost never say what they mean. Sometimes, a boy would much rather wander around whatever he wants you to know instead of saying exactly what he's thinking. Noah was no exception there.

I felt comfortable with Noah. It was what made him different. I'd never felt comfortable with Pierre. I'd never felt that comfortable with Louis Pamelville, who also once called me his girlfriend.

I wasn't comfortable with Noah just because he was weird, and I knew that I could take him in a fight with my left hand even if I had to do something else (like carve a turkey or dig a hole) with my right hand. The feeling of comfort made me want him to kiss me. I wanted Noah to kiss me.

Noah was quiet, staring at me like he was trying to stay completely still lest his brain explode in a giant blast of blood and skin. He leaned in just a little bit. He was close enough that I could smell his hair, which was vanilla-y. His mouth smelled like wintergreen gum. I may have closed my eyes at that point.

Noah moved in to kiss me. I don't know what it was exactly, but it suddenly did not feel right. It wasn't graceful. It wasn't perfect. He leaned in, and I took a step back.

"I'm sorry," he said.

"For what?"

"I get it."

"You get what?" I said.

"You want to be friends or something?"

"Yeah," I said. "I do want to be friends."

"I know. I get it. I've heard that song and dance before."

"I don't think you have," I said. I was feeling light-headed and shaky. My stomach was moving independently of my body. It was weird.

"I'm just sorry that I even put you in the position where you had to make that clear. Of course you just want to be friends."

"I don't *just* want to be friends." He was misunderstanding me. I hated being misunderstood. It's one of the best reasons not to talk to people. "It's not a second prize. I don't hand that out to everyone like it's money. I don't . . ."

"You don't what?"

"I never had any friends." That was probably the truest thing I'd ever said.

He was quiet for a moment. We turned to the side of the hedges that camouflaged the rocket ship from the rest of the estate. "Why me?"

I think what I said was, "Because I know you."

I saw him shake his head, and I think he said, "You don't know me at all." He looked off into space. "Astrid, I'm a liar."

And that was when I heard the splash. It was loud and angry. Like a piano falling into the middle of the ocean right next to me. Somehow, I knew what it was. I ran toward it as fast as I could.

# FRITZ

It was just a goddamn pool. It got deep, sure, but just seven feet. It was big, though. The pool was giant from end to end.

Thirty seconds had passed since I'd heard the splash. It felt like an hour, but it likely took us much less time than that to run fifty feet. Noah was an awkward runner, but he wasn't slow.

My grandfather's wheelchair lay on its side at the edge of the pool. One of the wheels—the little one up front—had somehow fallen off and now was bobbing in the middle of the pool. I turned to the pool and saw the skeletal figure of the Honorable Montgomery Krieger of Connecticut floating facedown. Grandpa wore the long sort of pajamas that men wore in silent movies. The kind with the butt flap.

There wasn't too much light out there, and when a cloud passed over the moon, my grandpa's floating figure

didn't look like a person at all. He wasn't shaking or struggling. He was just going down. Down into the water. And
as the figure moved farther underwater, I could make out
Grandpa's wrinkly, spotted, fat head. Grandpa wasn't trying to grab any air or anything. He was just going down.

Just going down.

We once had a summer compound near the Cape in
Massachusetts. My grandfather had a sailboat and there
was this guy, Captain Steve, and he was supposed to teach
us how to sail. My grandfather was disappointed that my
dad wasn't good with knots. He wanted to make sure that
Lisbet, Fritz, and I were knot prodigies. There is a ton
more involved in sailing, I have to assume, but as far as
we were concerned, the whole thing came down to knots.
It was boring. Lisbet cared. I didn't. Fritz didn't.

I think at that point, I was into fencing, or at least
I had this épée that I would carry around with me. I
liked to slice it through the air and point it at people and
make demands. Fritz wanted one too, and when he got
one, we would fence in the underneath part of the boat,
where there was a room and a bar and couches. "The
underneath part" is a technical sailboating term. Also,

the front of the boat is called the "bow" and the back of the boat is called the "back part." I was and am no expert on boats.

It began to rain, so I was perfectly fine staying in the underneath part to keep dry. Captain Steve or Something could pilot the boat to shore without my help. Fritz worried that there was no room down there for a proper fencing match. "I can't stab anything down here," he said. So he decided to take things upstairs.

I didn't want to go upstairs. I didn't want to get wet from the rain, and I didn't want to hear anything more about how to pilot a rig, or whatever sailors talked about. But there was really no way for me to prove my superiority as a fencer if I didn't see the end to that particular bout.

I climbed the stairs, tilted the trapdoor up, and stepped on the deck just in time to catch a bucketful of rain on my head and hear the splash and cry of Fritz falling into the water. I looked over the edge of the boat to see him hitting at the ocean with his palms first. He kept his head above for a little bit. The water was choppy from the storm and the waves pushed him farther away from the boat. And then he couldn't keep his head above the waves.

Noah knelt at the edge of the pool. He didn't move to jump into the water.

"Somebody? Hello! Somebody? Help!"

"Let me guess," I said. "You can't swim."

"I can't swim!" Noah's face was red, and he was beginning to look panicked. I stared at the water, feeling my body tremble.

"Can you swim?" Noah yelled.

"Yes! Of course!" But I didn't jump in. "I can . . . but I'm scared."

"You're not scared of anything! You said that!" His voice was getting increasingly louder with every word.

"Well, guess what? I'm a liar. I'm a liar, and I'm scared of water. Okay?" I was screaming at him by that point. "My brother's dead; my grandpa's in the pool. You can't swim. I'm scared, okay?"

"You're not a liar. You're not afraid of anything." Then he looked at me for a final second and said the thing I'd all but forgotten: "You're Astrid Krieger!"

"Call someone," I yelled. "Get help or something. Go!"

"What are you going to do?" Noah asked.

"I'm jumping in." And I jumped in as Noah ran to the front of the house, yelling for help.

>>>>>>>>>>>>>

There are these moments where you can't always figure out if you're doing the best thing. You just do the thing that happens. Does that make sense? Sometimes you don't actually make those little decisions at all: if you're going to take your shoes off before you jump in, if you're going to be able to pull him up, if you know what to do at all.

The water was cold, and it was hard to see under there. The pool lights were off most nights. I had to just wave my arms around until I felt something. Eventually I felt a limb. An arm. A leg, maybe. I wasn't sure. I didn't know how long I was under the water. A few seconds. A minute. I felt like I needed to breathe, but I also needed to grab and pull because my grandfather was drowning down there and no one else was there to do anything about it.

I hated the water.

I pulled at his leg, or his arm, or whatever, and I opened my eyes when I could breathe again. I felt around for the way back up and somehow managed to pull both my grandfather and myself over to the edge of the pool. I lifted myself out, over the stone, holding onto the senator's chest with my other arm while keeping his head above the surface. When I was completely out of the pool,

I could lean over the side and pull my grandfather's whole body to the concrete around the pool. I have no idea how I was able to do that.

I didn't know CPR, so I just pounded on Grandpa's chest. It seemed like the right thing to do. I pounded a few times, and I put my ear close to his mouth. I heard the sound of his shallow, raspy breathing. It wasn't a hearty, full, *I want to live, dammit!* cry, but it meant he was breathing. I breathed too. I laughed a little. It wasn't a perfect situation, but he'd been drowning, and then he was alive, and that's what the point of jumping in was.

I looked at the senator lying there, breathing his shallow breaths, and I couldn't help but think for a minute that the one I jumped in after—the one I saved—wasn't my grandfather at all. In my confused state, for a moment I believed it was Fritz that I'd pulled out of the water.

It had happened the same way with Fritz. I was the only one who could get to him. Everyone had been on the far side of the boat or underneath the main cabin. By the time they got there, Fritz was gone. I was the only one who could have jumped in and saved him. But I hadn't jumped in after Fritz. It had been raining, and there were waves, and the boat was moving fast, and more importantly, I just didn't. I didn't used to be afraid of the water, but I was after that. I saw Fritz go under, and he never came up again.

# CHAPTER 22

# DRIVING LESSONS

There are a lot of places to go in a hospital if you don't want to be found. I chose a room where a woman was recovering from having things shoved in her boobs and stuffed in her lips. It wasn't pretty (which I'm sure was the opposite of her intention). She didn't want me in the room, but she was unable to actually tell me to leave (because of the stuff in her lips). It was for the best. In the future—advice to everyone—if there's a wet girl in a fancy dress covered in mud and scratches, with eye makeup running down her face and neck, and she's sitting in your hospital room, leave it alone. Let whatever happens happen.

I sat there quietly for a while. The lady in the room tried to say something, possibly, "Are you okay?" She said it in between her gross lips, though, so she could've been saying anything. I was okay.

Hours before, I'd been in the ambulance with my

grandfather. I was yelling at him. I was yelling as loud as I could. "Did you jump in the pool? What were you trying to do? You knew you wouldn't be able to get yourself out. What if I hadn't come home? Who was going to help you? What were you trying to do? Was it on purpose?"

Grandpa answered in an uncharacteristically quiet voice: "Puppy, it's just . . . the world turned and flung me." Then he laughed and wheezed and coughed this horrible sound, like he was spitting up a mouthful of needles.

He didn't want to tell me why he jumped in the pool. I never found out whether or not he did it on purpose. I can't say I'm positive he was trying to die, but an elderly man who can't move his legs usually doesn't get that close to a pool.

His only answer was that the world had flung him. He made an excuse. He laid out an alibi. He told me it was the world's fault.

The other thing I kept thinking about was what Noah had said: "He told me that you've turned out better than he could ever be." Something about that felt weird. And not just because that wasn't my grandfather's style.

I walked out to the lobby; I was still dripping wet, a fact that everyone kept noticing and pointing out. If the members of my family all had one thing in common, it was real A+ skill in noticing whether or not someone was dry and pointing it out as if it were news. "Did you know you're wet, Astrid?" they all said. Then Vivi said, "I'm glad you're okay," but she probably thought that's what she was supposed to say.

Noah was fiddling with the Coke machine around the corner from the lobby. There was something I'd figured out, and I knew it was time to confront him.

"You knew my grandfather," I said.

"You must be freezing," he said.

"You worked there, right?"

As I wandered through the hospital to the Botox lady's room earlier, I saw a male nurse banging on a copy machine, fighting a paper jam in front of a tower of manila folders of records. At that instant, in my memory, I could see Noah doing pretty much the same thing. He was in a dress shirt and nice pants. I'd seen him at a photocopy machine and at a coffee machine. He'd been in an office. And I'd been in that office. He was copying a—what was it—a check or something.

"Yes," he said. He looked pained, like he'd been punched in the face.

"You met my grandfather before. He said of course he knew you. And you used to work for my father."

"It's not what you think."

"It's not? Because I think you weren't supposed to be at my high school at all. I think you work for my family. And you came there because it was part of your job. Someone paid you to go to Cadorette. To keep an eye on me. Did my family pay you to be my friend?"

"Okay. It's, um . . . it's what you think. But you don't understand. Let me explain . . . "

And then I felt something wet running down my face. I was crying, just like anyone else in the world might have done in that moment. I couldn't talk, I was shaking so much. Everything hurt so much.

"Sit down," Noah whispered. He took off his jacket and draped it around my shoulders. Then he let one of his hands linger on my shoulder.

"No!" I said. "Don't touch me. You're a liar."

"I know. That's what I said."

And then I paused for a long time, trying to catch my breath. The tears just kept on coming. I hated crying. I avoided it at all costs. But it was a release. It made me feel better. I started to see the appeal. "Why is everyone who likes me either fake or dead? Huh?"

And then I could finally purge myself of what I'd been crying about in the first place. "I don't want him to die, Noah."

Noah leaned in to hold me again, which was the wrong

move because when he got close enough, I punched him in the face.

BAM!

He flew back against the Coke machine. He raised his hands in front of his face to cover it, but I was able to get around them. I only stopped when I felt one of the hospital security guards pull me away. Even then, I probably connected a few more.

"You know, I trusted you," I said. "And I don't trust anyone."

>>>>>>>>>>>>

I wanted to get away. There was no reason I needed to sit in a hospital all night. In my hand were Noah's car keys from his suit jacket. I hadn't even noticed I'd grabbed them until I had them in my hand. And I must've had them in my hand the whole time I was hitting him. It had probably made it hurt more, and I was okay with that.

I found Noah's big-penis car and opened the door. Driving couldn't be that hard. I thought of all the people who managed to do it every single day. Most of those people had to have been idiots because most people *were* idiots. I put the key in the ignition and turned. It was easy. I had no idea why I hadn't tried it before. Then I moved the thing next to the thing. You know, that thing you pull to move from Park to Drive. I managed that with no problem.

And one second later:

SLAM!

The car hit the bumper of an ambulance. It made a loud crunching sound. That was pretty much the end of my driving career.

I got out of the car and immediately was blinded by a lot of bright lights. I couldn't see what was behind them, but they were moving at me. Running at me. Maybe ten of them, all white. It was only when they were practically touching my face that I could see where they were coming from. The lights belonged to television cameras. There were a million things happening that night, and now some stupid reporter was going to turn my collision with an ambulance into news. Goddamn news. What a worthless idea. Why would I be news to anyone?

"I did it," I said. "I hit an ambulance. There. Are you all happy?"

A woman in a business suit put a microphone in front of my face. I had to squint to even tell what it was. I couldn't see the woman's face. She could have been deformed, for all I saw. She could've had a giant Cyclops eye, which would've been awesome. She said, "How are you going to remember your grandfather?"

"What?" I asked. It was not me at my most quotable.

"Montgomery Krieger's death has affected people all over the country. All over the world. But he was your grandfather. What would you like people to know about him?"

That was how I found out. I didn't have the time to think about what I wanted people to know about him. He wasn't a good man, but the Kriegers aren't good people. I always thought he wanted me to be just like him, but it turned out *he* no longer wanted to be just like him, so he placed himself alone and helpless in the middle of a giant kidney-shaped pool. That's not what I told the news, though. I just said, "He's . . . he's dead?" Then the tears started again. I couldn't last five minutes in my plan to never cry again.

The camera tilted down, and I could see the reporter's face. She had a lousy stupid job to do, but I don't think she had planned to break that kind of news to me. She put the microphone down and quietly said, "I'm sorry." And then she hugged me. This stranger hugged me into her shoulder. She was probably a mother. A good one, unlike the one I was familiar with. I got snot all over her jacket, and she didn't even care.

She turned to the other reporters and said, "Not now, guys." The newspeople turned around, and all the bright white lights went away.

>>>>>>>>>>>>>

I wasn't on some search for how to change my life. I didn't read books about it. In fact, I wasn't reading books at all. This was the first book I ever finished reading—the book you are reading right now.

I wasn't looking for change, because I'd always liked who I was. I'd been called a lot of horrible things in my life, but it never really made a difference to me because I have always been pretty much thrilled with myself. That makes me different from probably ninety-nine point nine-nine-nine-nine percent of other seventeen-year-olds. I don't know a lot of other people my age that well, but I can just tell that they all pretty much hate themselves. Every morning they look in the mirror and they take a deep breath and all they can do is think about how much they want to vomit at their own reflections.

*I hate that I'm so fat and I have so many pimples and my breath stinks and I'm not very smart or I am too smart and no one likes someone who's too smart and my feet are big and I'm super gay and everyone hates this dress*, they might say. Is that about right? I'm guessing, but I think that's pretty much what most seventeen-year-old people say to themselves.

Not me, though.

I'd always woken up every morning and looked in the mirror, or one of many mirrors that I had hanging around (yeah, I had a lot of mirrors), and I thought about how great it was that I was Astrid Krieger. I'd always thought I was pretty lucky on that point. It was about as great as you would think it would be. Which was pretty great.

But for the first time, I wondered if I was wrong about myself.

The only light I saw apart from the hospital, which was lit pretty well, was a little orange glow under the emergency room awning. It was Vivi and her cigarette. I walked toward that beacon.

"Do you want to take a walk?" she asked when I'd joined her on the bench she was sitting on.

Although I didn't particularly want to, I nodded. We circled the parking lot together.

"Is that the boy's car?" she wanted to know.

"Yes. But I'm sure he's earned a new one. I hope Grandpa paid up before he kicked it."

"Why can't you ever make things easy, Astrid?"

"I try to make things as easy as I can."

"For yourself. Not for anyone else."

I'd heard that argument before, but it had been a while since I'd heard it from Vivi. "I've changed."

She laughed. "You should probably be out of range of the stolen car when you try to convince me you've changed."

"I have changed. I've done all sorts of good things. A list of them. An actual list, for Dean Rein. I may have done bad things in my day. But I am not a bad person."

"We're all bad people, Astrid. Every one of us."

I disagreed, but Vivi shared my penchant for making ridiculous statements, so I let it go. "Why don't we ever talk like this anymore?" she wanted to know. She started another one of her menthol cigarettes.

"We never talked, period."

"No. We talked. Things used to be different." I knew my mother well enough to know that sentence was close as she would ever come to telling me she cared or to talking about the bad things we were going through. I mean, if Fritz was actually named Things Used to Be Different Krieger, we would have talked about him all the time instead of, you know, never.

"Your grandfather didn't hire that boy to hurt you," she said.

I was glad we weren't going to pretend for the rest of our lives that someone wasn't paid to go with me to the homecoming dance. Because that's not something that happened to everyone.

"Sure," I said. "Whatever."

"It's true. He's been sick for a long time, you know. He wanted to have someone looking out for you."

"I can look out for myself."

"Don't I know it. Monty said you would figure it out in the end."

"Not fast enough."

"Well, he bet me a thousand bucks that you would put it together. Now that you did, though, I don't have to pay him. Because he's dead. Good for me. I'm sorry. Gallows humor. I used to work in a hospital."

"I'm sure you were hilarious, Vivi."

"Don't be sarcastic. It gives you face lines."

"Why did he do it, then? Why did he hire Noah?"

"Probably because you get away with everything. You make messes. We can't trust you, Astrid. We never know what phone call we're going to get next. We have to live our lives."

"You live your lives all the time. Everyone lives their lives. And that's all I want. Let me live my life."

Vivi laughed. "When have I stopped you from living your life however you wanted? My head hurts from you living your life however you want. You're almost eighteen. You're almost your own problem. In a few months, you're free to dig your own ditch and fall in it."

"It's victory enough just to have you rooting for me, Vivi."

"This family can't solve your problems forever," she said.

"When have you ever solved my problems? When has anyone in this family solved anything without throwing money at it?"

"Money solves some problems. You've used that method yourself."

"You know," I said, "Grandpa tried to pay Randy not to marry Lisbet."

Vivi smiled slightly. "Of course I know that. He tried to pay me not to marry your father. He makes the offer to everyone. If it works, good riddance."

I frowned, feeling a familiar tightness in my chest. It bothered me that Grandpa had tricks I didn't know about.

She sighed and rubbed her temples. "What do you want?"

"I want to go back to Bristol," I said.

"I never wanted you out of Bristol. They asked you to leave."

"You and Dad made me go to public school."

"That wasn't us," she said. "That was your grandfa-ther's idea too. We would be perfectly fine sending you off to wherever you wanted. But Montgomery thought you could learn something from the experience."

I just stared. Was she lying? Why would she lie? What would her endgame be? She had to be telling the truth because the lie wasn't going to get her anything.

"I want to go back to Bristol," I repeated.

"I thought you liked it at the public school. I thought you had friends."

"I was wrong." I felt myself tearing up again. It was really embarrassing.

"Okay," she agreed. "If that's what you want."

# CHAPTER 23

# MY BOYFRIEND

**I** had been back at Bristol for a month. It was what I'd wanted, which I guessed was a good thing.

When Vivi called Dean Rein shortly after my grandfather died and asked him to take me back, he reminded her that the decision didn't belong to my family; it belonged to him. He was the one who had expelled me. They went back and forth for a few phone calls, but he suddenly relented, provided that I sit down with him again to show him my list.

That list.

I guess I couldn't really expect to get my old life back without it, but at that point, even looking at that stupid piece of paper made me feel a little squeamish. Somehow my list still smelled like Cadorette Township High School. I mean, there I was at Bristol, which smelled like freshly cut grass and diamond earrings, but in my hand was this yellow piece of paper from another planet that smelled like . . . herpes medicine and body odor?

Dean Rein put on his reading glasses because he really wanted me to know he was taking this seriously. He rocked back and forth in his chair. He was silent for a full five minutes. I don't think he'd ever been silent for five minutes. In his sleep, he probably talked about his stupid skiing vacations.

"Subtracting the ones I already discounted, we're left with two," he said.

"There were five on the list. You crossed out two. That's three."

"Telling me to shove it up my ass does not suit the purposes of this challenge."

"It was still fun to put down," I said.

"You helped that girl become homecoming queen. And saved your sister from heartbreak on her wedding day. These two are good."

"I know. Really good. Great, even."

"Too bad you didn't have three."

"Too bad, indeed."

"But you *did* do three good things." He had this stupid grin on his face, like he was telling me a secret. I wanted to punch him so hard. "I watch the news. You saved your grandfather's life."

"My grandfather's dead. So, your sources are inaccurate."

"I'm sorry for your loss."

"Thanks," I mumbled.

"The intent matters. You did it naturally. You did it in the moment. I'll give you credit for it. If it's what you want."

It felt weird to use that thing that happened in the pool as something to bargain with. I didn't jump in the pool for any real reason. I just happened not to be a monster. If someone else saw that as a good deed, then that was fine. All I really had to do was nod, and I could get back into Bristol. And that's what I wanted. I was pretty sure that's what I wanted. So I said, "Fine. Then count it. Three good things."

He peered at the list in his hand once more. "In the end, the list . . . it was a pretty good idea."

I shrugged. "Sure."

"I was skeptical at first, of course, about being your therapist at all. However, you can't really get hung up on what's conventional. Not if you have a solution that might work."

I wasn't following, which usually happened when I spoke with Dean Rein because I usually zoned out and lost track of the conversation.

"Why are you acting like none of this was your idea?"
I said. "It wasn't *my* idea. I didn't want any of this."

"It wasn't my idea, Astrid. I thought you knew?"

"Knew what?"

"It was your grandfather's idea. I'm sorry. I hope this
doesn't upset you."

I didn't even know if I could be upset anymore. First
Noah, then public school, now Dean Rein and the list.
It was all my grandfather. He'd wanted something more
from me. I didn't know what. I bit my lip hard. I wasn't
upset. I didn't have the energy anymore.

I guess that's how I would describe what it was like to
be back at Bristol. I just didn't have the energy. Somehow
Pierre understood that, which was weird because Pierre
usually didn't understand anything. I'd definitely seen him
regard a zipper like it was a supercomputer.

Pierre came back to Bristol around the same time I did.
I wasn't surprised. It would have been strange if he hadn't
come back. He didn't speak to me for three days. This was
a conscious effort on his part, I'm sure. I wasn't broken up
about it. I didn't really notice.

The fourth day, I saw him sitting on a bench as I
walked by. When I was almost all the way past him, he
said, "So this is how we meet again." This would have
worked better if I'd been looking at him, but the point

was made. He was waiting for me, and he'd forced me to notice.

I turned around and shuffled back over to where he was sitting. I had this image in my mind that everywhere I walked for the rest of the year, he would be sitting, waiting for me. Waiting for me to look at him and talk to him. I couldn't deal with it. He had something he wanted to say, and I couldn't think of a good reason to continue putting it off. "Pierre, what? What can I help you with? Tell me what you want from me, already. Just tell me."

I don't think he was expecting that sort of reaction. I don't think he had any answer for me. He liked chasing me. He thought it was romantic that he was always behind me and I was always running away. I didn't think it was romantic. It was a very unpleasant reminder of why it wasn't always good to be liked.

Pierre appeared to be thinking hard about what he was going to say. He was probably weighing whether or not to read me a poem or play me a song or write my name in clumps of grass. Wisely, he threw out all of those ideas. "Have dinner with me. We can go wherever you want. We can go into New York if you'd like. We can get on a plane if that is what you want. But have dinner with me."

"Okay," I was shocked to hear myself say. I wasn't

sure where that word actually came from or why it was in my mouth. "But let's go somewhere close."

Pierre suggested dinner at the restaurant that pretended it was the fifties. And even though I hated the very idea of that place, I also hated the very idea of having dinner with Pierre. Since I had already agreed to that, I figured (as my grandfather would have said), *If you're already served a shit sandwich, you might as well top it with more shit.*

During this dinner, Pierre asked me if I would be his girlfriend. He'd called me his girlfriend for a long time, but I'd never agreed. This time I said yes. Please do not throw this book across the room in anger. As soon as we got to the restaurant—or whatever it was, since *restaurant* is a word they use for places that serve excellent food, but this place had waitresses singing doo-wop music—the first thing I made Pierre do was tell the waitstaff to refrain from any more of their songs. And he convinced them. First, they were like, "It's our job." But Pierre mumbled something to them and pointed at me, and they all looked a little scared, and they didn't sing again.

Pierre might have a ponytail. He might have a completely ridiculous interest in porcelain statues of angel children. (Because, he said, "They are experiencing a perfect eternity every day.") He might wear pants that look like bathroom wallpaper. But here's the thing: he was always nice to me.

By the time I got back to Bristol, I was completely out of people who were nice to me. Noah had turned out to be a spy. My grandfather had hired Noah. My parents knew about it.

Pierre talked a lot about love while we were together. It was basically how he started the conversation that night at dinner. He said, "The thing is this: I know you hate me to say this. You said that you hate it. But I can't help saying it again: I love you, Astrid. That is it. That is all. If I cannot be with you . . . I don't know. I can't do anything about it, but I can ask."

I didn't want to argue with him. But I could accept that it was less about him and whether he could love me than about the idea of love itself. Perhaps he loved me as much as someone could. But the more I thought about love, I felt less and less that love itself was real. Human beings have been around for a long time, and we have all sorts of things that have changed over the years to make it better for us to survive. Like eyebrows. And thumbs. And love, if it is real, is the sort of thing that should have evolved away. Love leads to people jumping in front of moving trains. You know, like, *If you don't love me back, I will let this train run me over.* Or, *That person I am married to is about to get hit by that train. So, I will get hit by that train instead. SPLAT.* That sort of thing happens.

"I'm just going to say this," I said to Pierre. "I don't love you. I don't think I will ever love you. I am not trying to be mean. I am just telling the truth. I don't think I can love people."

Pierre thought about this. "Is this because of that other boy? That Noah?" I was pretty sure that it had nothing to do with Noah. With Noah, maybe I had become temporarily a little dumb because I liked him. But I didn't turn into Lisbet or anything. I didn't picture a big house for me and Noah filled with our babies dressed in little versions of his polyester shirts. I didn't write my name in a notebook with his last name . . . if the last name he'd given me was even real. Astrid J. Krieger-Einstein. Ugh, that just sounded horrible. That name in itself was a train about to run me over. I just thought he was cute, and I liked how he smelled, and I didn't think it through beyond that.

"No," I said. "It has nothing to do with him. It just has to do with who I am."

He looked down at his pancakes. That was what he was eating for dinner: pancakes. "I think I understand. I think it is very clear. But I don't need you to be in love with me. That is okay. I just want you to be my girlfriend. I am sure it would be not too terrible for you to have somebody to eat dinner with. To have someone to sit with in class. To have someone to give you rides." Pierre was pretty much offering what he did for me anyway. He just wanted to name the thing. For whatever reason, it was important to him to use the title. The word *girlfriend* meant something to him. And it meant nothing to me, so what was I doing fighting it? It was like someone asking you for your cake when you'd already dropped it on the floor. You weren't going to eat it, so why not give it up?

"Fine," I said. "I'll be your girlfriend. But not a lot of kissing or anything, please."

Pierre smiled. I didn't particularly understand why he wanted it, but he got what he wanted.

>>>>>>>>>>>>

I never felt super comfortable calling Pierre my boyfriend. I don't know if I actually ever said the sentence *That's my boyfriend, Pierre,* aloud. But what I called it wasn't the point.

I found out quickly that one of the main reasons Pierre wanted to formally be my boyfriend was because he wanted people to know. He wanted people to see the two of us walking together and for them to think they understood something about our relationship. He wanted people to know him as Pierre, Astrid Krieger's boyfriend. Or, you know, whatever his actual name was, followed by "Astrid Krieger's boyfriend." To his surprise, about ninety-nine point nine-nine-nine percent of people couldn't have cared less about whom he was dating or that I was his girlfriend. When it all came down to it, only one other person really cared. And she cared a lot.

Talia Pasteur was angry.

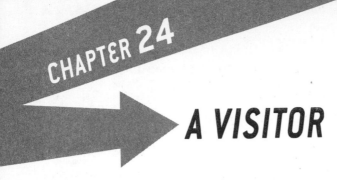

# CHAPTER 24

# A VISITOR

**I** didn't know if I was going to have to wait a week, a month, a year. As it turned out, a mere day after I agreed to allow Pierre to use the word *girlfriend*, I walked into my room to find Talia sitting on the edge of my bed.

Talia's hair was now short in the back, parted, and combed up on one side. If it hadn't been an unnatural white-blond color, it would have been the exact same haircut as my dad's. She circled the room and took a glass off my dresser, then dropped it on the floor. "Whoops," she said. It didn't crash as elegantly as Talia had probably hoped it would. It bounced off the floor and chipped.

"That isn't mine," I told her. Actually, almost nothing in the room was mine. I had sheets, clothes, and a small refrigerator for my juice boxes. Almost everything else of importance I'd left back on the rocket ship.

"Why did you come back here?" Talia said.

I shrugged. "I was never supposed to leave."

"Of course you were."

"Just because you wanted me to leave doesn't mean I was supposed to," I said.

"You were a terrible person. You did all sorts of terrible things. They should've kicked you out a long time ago."

"I'm not a terrible person," I said, although I wasn't sure how much I completely believed it anymore. "I was never terrible to you."

"Of course you were. Every single day. You kept telling me how much I looked like a tree."

"You *did* look like a tree."

"I'm not finished, Astrid. You made me hate myself. You took the one thing I wanted in the world." She didn't want to say Pierre's name aloud and that was fine because I never liked to say his actual name either, given the phlegm that accompanied the act of pronouncing it. She was of course in love with him, and I was more than fine with that. They could move back to Bratislava or wherever he was from. I wasn't stopping them.

I never thought of myself as being mean to Talia, but maybe I had been. I didn't like her. At that point, I probably hated her. Maybe I'd always been terrible to her.

"You have the only thing I ever wanted in the world, and you didn't even have to try. You don't even really want it." She was trying very hard to look at me with cold eyes, but they were getting red and watery.

"He is the only thing you ever wanted in the world?"

"Not just him. Everything. You're so pretty, and you're so rich, and people listen to you even if you're mean to them, and everyone has always done everything you wanted them to do. You have all of that, and you've never, ever even cared."

"Don't you have all that now? Isn't everyone at school terrified of you?"

"They're terrified of me, but they don't admire me. And still, it's hard work. I have to try every day."

"So that's why you set me up?" I said. "Because I don't try hard enough?"

"Set you up?" She asked it as if she didn't understand any of the words. "You keep saying that. You cheated. You weren't set up."

"We all cheated. Someone sold me out, though. And that person was you."

"Why would you be so sure it was me?"

"Wasn't it you?"

"You can't prove anything," she said. She had a point. "You can't do anything anymore. I filled the power vacuum when you left and there's no more room for you. Nobody's going to help you."

"You know, we *were* kind of friends, Talia. Maybe that's why I'm mad at you. Because I sort of liked you. I thought you were like me."

"It turns out I never really liked you."

"Get off it. Don't all friends go through the 'I never liked you' stage?"

Talia shook her head. "No one likes you. No one wants you to be here. Lukas said that no one even liked you at the other school." Apparently Pierre had been talking about me to Talia. Which was awesome. I was so glad I had a boyfriend. "You're all alone, and nobody likes you," she said. "I just want to make sure you know that."

Apparently satisfied that I knew it now, Talia got up off the bed and walked slowly out the door, knocking another glass on the floor as she went.

"That one's not mine either," I called after her.

As Talia had said, I was all alone. I'd been all alone a lot. For most of my life. I'd almost always chosen to be that way. But I didn't want to be all by myself anymore. Alas, it's hard to choose *not* to be alone.

The next few weeks, I went into hiding. I wasn't hiding from anyone in particular; I just didn't want anyone to see me. I slept a lot. I felt like I was catching up on sleep I had spent years missing. I woke up one morning to the phone ringing. I didn't know how long it was ringing. I didn't even know the dorm rooms had phones. "Hello?"

"This is security." Security was a new thing at Bristol. Part of it was related to me, but also one of the princes of Jordan was a student, and so they put an old guy who was barely coherent in a uniform and sat him in front of the main entrance. That way, if an international assassin were to break into the school, he might be asked to show ID. He mumbled something about how I had a visitor and asked whether it was okay to send him through.

I didn't want a visitor. I didn't want anyone near me. "He says he's from your other school," the guard said. I had told myself a hundred times that I never, ever wanted to see Noah again. But you can't lie to yourself forever, which is why I smiled. I smiled like a drunk five-year-old.

"Can I send him over?" the security guard wanted to know.

Before I could change my mind, I said, "Please do."

For the next five minutes, I went through every emotion available to me. I landed somewhere in between nervous and thirsty. I practiced telling him, *Die, asshole,* and slamming the door in his face, and I practiced saying, *Hi, I'm glad it was you.* I figured I would do whatever felt most natural. Then there was a knock, and I opened the door.

I said neither of those things because it wasn't Noah behind the door. It was Mason. And behind him was Lucy. When Lucy saw me, her mouth opened so wide that her hair fell out and returned to the side of her head where it belonged. All she said was, "You don't look good at all."

>>>>>>>>>>>>

Lucy would not stop talking.

It was about five minutes until I could even figure out why she and Mason were at Bristol at all, and that was only because I actually stopped to ask her. She had gone kind of nuts.

In my room that day, she was pacing around like my cousin Crispin before he takes his pills. Or like my cousin Gunther after he takes Crispin's pills. She had this look in her eyes. It wasn't crazy, but it was intense. "I've been meaning to come up here for weeks and weeks and I'm sorry. I've been trying, and I'm really sorry," Lucy said.

"She's been meaning to. She kept saying it," Mason said.

"I know. I know," she said. "I've been like, 'When are we going to see Astrid? Can we go up to Astrid's school today?' And then my mom's car—she was in an accident; she's fine. She was parked. But the car . . . And then—"

"I don't have a car. I use my brother's and he needs it for work."

"Mason's brother has to drive to work, right. And then the days, they turned into weeks. And then I just looked at Mason this morning and I said, it's been a month. Can you believe it? It's been a whole month. I said, 'I don't care how we do it. I'm just not going to be able to live with myself if we don't go up there today.'"

"We took the bus."

"Two buses and a taxi. It's not the easiest place to find."

"There were cows. There were a lot of cows."

"I know. But we're here. Finally. Phew."

Lucy stopped talking. She sat down on my desk chair and caught her breath. I continued to have no idea what the hell she was talking about, but I did notice that as she and Mason were having this back-and-forth tennis match of a conversation, her weird lisp had disappeared. I had understood everything she said, even though I didn't understand why she was saying it. And also, Lucy looked entirely different without actually looking very different at all. She was wearing the same sort of lumpy clothes she'd worn before, and her hair was the same, but she was kind of colorful looking. She showed her teeth more, and occasionally she would brush her hand across Mason's hand. And when she was sitting, Mason would lightly tap her. They both had moments of silence when they would look at each other and not say anything, and then they would nod as if communicating telepathically. I guess I had kept my promise to Lucy. Maybe Lucy and Mason were in love. It was sweet. It was *disgusting*. But still, sweet.

They were both looking at me like it was my turn. It was as though I'd asked them to show up, and we had planned out this whole day, and I was supposed to play some sort of part at that point.

"Lucy. Mason. Let me just say, thank you for coming. But I have absolutely no idea what you're talking about. Why did you come here?" I said.

Lucy blinked a few times, then looked at Mason and then looked back at me. I couldn't tell if I'd hurt her feelings or she was just as confused by my reaction as I was by the conversation. She said, "Mason was right. That's what he said. He said you were going to have no idea what we're talking about. But I just, I just thought that was totally ridiculous. I just knew. But I guess I didn't know."

"It's not a big deal," Mason said.

"Should we go?" she asked. "We should go." Lucy was suddenly the fastest person in the world since she'd walked into my room, so she was almost out the door before I could respond.

"No," I said. "You don't have to go."

Lucy took a deep breath and settled back into the chair. "I just couldn't figure out why you left our school. Then I heard that you came back here and I thought, oh, of course. That makes total sense. You must have a plan."

"A plan for what?" I said.

"You know," Lucy said.

"I don't."

"Because you're back here."

"Yeah, because . . ." Mason said.

"What plan?" I asked again.

"It's why we came," Lucy said. "We assumed you needed help. You did something great for us, and so we needed to help. To return the favor."

"Seriously. What plan?"

"Well, of course . . ." Lucy said. "For revenge?"

# CHAPTER 25

# SHARK SMILES

"We never meet like this anymore. It's a real shame." When I came back to Bristol, Dean Rein and I both decided that I should no longer be enrolled in his class. He felt it was a conflict of interest. I told him that was fine because if I had to keep seeing him regularly, I might put a letter opener up my nose. So he was nothing to me. I wasn't cheating anymore, and he knew that because my grades were awful. I only had to see him in the morning during chapel and whenever we would pass each other on campus, and he would smile, and I would not smile in return.

"Why is it a shame? Did you miss me?" I asked.

Dean Rein had said that his door was always open, which is something people say even if (like Dean Rein) they don't mean it at all. His door was never open. I had to sit outside his office for ten minutes while his secretary, Beth, figured out whether he was actually in his office. She didn't like me. But if I were to go by what she had taped to her computer, the only things she liked were comic strips about trying on swimsuits, so I didn't take it personally. "My weeks have been a lot less exciting without our sessions. Boring even. I've had too many consecutive days without a student telling me my head is misshapen. And we were making some real progress, weren't we?"

"Sure. Totally." I leaned in. "I actually need your help."

I knew how happy it must have made Dean Rein to hear me asking for help. I did not like making him happy. "I'm here because I had no one else to talk to. I just want to make sure you know that up front. If there was anyone in the entire world I could talk to right now instead of you, I would do that."

"Understood. I know this must be difficult for you to come to me. But I'm listening." He was still smiling.

"I'm . . . " I had to breathe between words. "I'm worried about what people think of me," I said.

"Why?"

"I've changed, right? I mean, since all that stuff happened at the beginning of the school year, and then when I did the good things and . . . I mean, I'm back here at Bristol, aren't I? I've changed."

Dean Rein took another sip from his mug. "You and I

have never gotten along," he said. "I think we could both agree on that. I would be the first person to doubt any changes you've made." He thought about it a little more. "But I don't. I think you've made a lot of strides. I'm very proud of the person you've become."

"Thank you," I said.

"So, what is this about?" he said. "Why the urgency?"

I told him about Lucy and Mason's visit. I told him about how after I basically changed their stupid lives, they still came here because they expected the Astrid Krieger they knew to have some sort of giant revenge plan brewing. "So, what's the point?" I said. "No matter what I do, nobody thinks of me as anything except this lousy person who's just out to hurt people."

"Revenge for what?"

"What do you mean?"

"They thought you had a revenge plan. What would you be seeking revenge for?"

"Oh . . . you know . . . When I was kicked out of here before, they thought I was planning on doing something to whoever set me up."

"Set you up? Ah, this business again."

"I don't really think I need to go into how it went down. But I know you were manipulated, and I'm okay with it," I said.

Dean Rein was smirking again. "I'm curious. How do you think I was manipulated?"

"I mean, it's not important or anything," I said. "But, you know, because somebody told you that I was the one who broke into your office, and then that person sent you those tests. I certainly wasn't, you know, the world's most honest student or anything—"

"Yes, you could say that."

"But I wasn't the only cheater. Cheating is wrong. I know that now. It was bigger than me. But someone tipped you off about only me. The person who did that might deserve some retribution. At least that's what Mason and Lucy suggested. It was probably Talia Pasteur, but you don't have to confirm that."

Dean Rein's smile broke off into a full, long, ridiculously loud fake laugh. I thought he was going to tip out of his chair and hit his head on his desk, which would be the worst injury anyone had ever sustained from a fake laugh. "Not that it matters, but nobody set you up, Astrid. Not Talia. Not anyone."

"Okay," I said.

"I didn't get an email from some anonymous source letting me know when and where you would be cheating. I knew you would be cheating because I pay attention. I figured it out. I made you think someone sent me those tests, but I found them myself. It was me. I knew you were going to cheat on my test, and I caught you. So, if you were going to enact revenge on someone—"

"I'm not."

"The person who set you up was me."

"Okay," I said.

"So, am I safe? Should I fear vengeance? Do I have to worry about toilet paper all over my car?" Dean Rein predictably used as boring a prank imaginable as an example.

"You certainly don't have to worry about me papering your car. Or anything, you know, *more interesting*. I'm not looking for that. Not from you. Not from anyone. I just don't care anymore," I said.

"That's a big step, Astrid. Aren't both of our lives so much easier without all of the distraction of this . . . ?" He made two fists and knocked them together. One of the fists was supposed to represent him, and the other one was supposed to be me. If I was a wrinkly, clenched, old-man hand. "Aren't our lives better without the headaches?"

"Absolutely."

And that's when we both heard the screaming.

First it was just this loud wail coming from right under Dean Rein's window. It didn't sound like anything coming from a person. But I could just make out words. "MY LEG!" and "THE HORSE!"

Dean Rein looked at me as if for some sort of confirmation that we were both hearing the same thing, and then he kicked over his chair and ran to the window. "No. No. Not again," he muttered.

"Stay here," he shouted when he was almost out the door. "I'll be . . . Stay here!"

I didn't have to look out the window because I knew what I would see. There would be a tall boy sprawled on the ground. Nobody at Bristol would recognize him, but he'd look like he belonged there. He'd be wearing a Bristol blazer. No one would look at his face. If they did, they would see details that might have seemed out of place. His hair was curly and dyed black, but it was pushed forward, so all you could see were his teeth clenched in pain. He wore chipped black nail polish on his fingers. His belt was made from the drawstring for the curtains in my dorm room because the belt he'd been wearing earlier was covered in spikes. Nobody would see any of that. All they would see was the blood. There would be a lot of blood. Blood on his shirt. Blood on his face. Blood all over the rips in his pants. Yeah, there would be a lot of blood. Of course, he didn't feel anything. Although he was screaming about a horse running over his leg, he wasn't in any pain.

There was a simple explanation for this. A horse *didn't* run over his leg. He wasn't covered in blood. He wasn't even a student at Bristol. The mixture of soap and an entire case of raspberry juice boxes that covered Mason looked so much like blood that I wished I could take credit for it. But that detail was Mason's idea. He had an intimate knowledge of the texture and components of fake blood. He was out there because I told him to be there. And he was doing a pretty good job, from what it sounded like. Up until that morning, I'd had no plan. This plan—the new plan—was going pretty well so far.

My meeting with Dean Rein went exactly the way I'd wanted it to. He managed to give me every piece of information I needed without realizing he'd given me anything. By telling me that no one set me up and no one tipped him off, he'd managed to prove the opposite was true. His tell was that he complimented himself for figuring it all out on his own. I knew he wasn't the sort of person who could figure something like that out by himself. Maybe I was a cheater, but I'd been a cheater for a long time, and he'd never before noticed a thing. He wanted me to think he was smart. That's why he brought it up. He didn't even notice that he told me how he was tipped off—by an anonymous email. I'm very glad that I never conspired with Dean Rein to rob a bank or anything because I would be in prison.

I sat at his desk in front of his computer. It was password protected, but that part wasn't difficult. It is very hard to guess a smart person's password because it should have nothing to do with anything. My computer password this very second is tuxedohamburgerduckcancer-9943**12. And twenty seconds after I just typed it out, I changed it, so don't even bother. People who aren't very smart will usually just use something they like. Lisbet's password is *rainbows*. My father's password is *eyebrows*. From what I knew about Dean Rein, it was pretty easy to guess what the thing he liked more than anything else in the world was. Dean Rein's password was, of course, *deanrein*.

I knew what I was looking for, but I wasn't exactly sure what I would find. I was looking for a specific email. An email about me—but that was all I knew.

Everything Lucy said that morning had been right. She was much more observant than I'd expected her to be. She'd listened to everything I ever said to her. Maybe I could've listened to everything she ever said to me if it wasn't so damn hard to understand her. What she heard was that I would never be okay with Talia Pasteur getting me kicked out of school. Anyone who was involved needed to know that there were consequences. I needed to do something. I'd changed a lot in the past few months, and I was happy about being a better person, but that didn't mean I should abandon what was right. Talia Pasteur deserved whatever was going to happen to her. The part of me that was going to make that happen? Well, that was a part that I felt should never change. I couldn't get past this feeling that my grandfather had died disappointed in me. He made all this happen, and I didn't know of any other reason he would have for punishing me. Maybe I was disappointing. I should never have been the sort of person that lets things happen to her.

Finding the emails was remarkably easy. The anonymous tipster was blackmailing Dean Rein with some information he needed to stay a secret. It actually wasn't a big deal: Dean Rein's son, Martin Jr. (the one who blew his arm off in the meth explosion), stole fifty thousand dollars from the Bristol beautification fund and lost it betting on a football game. Dean Rein had replaced the money by taking out a second mortgage on his house, and he hoped that nobody would ever find out.

Joe Flemming had already discovered this while looking through computer records. He had told me, Pierre, Talia Pasteur, and (I think) Peter Elfrish. I knew I could probably use that information against Dean Rein. It might even put him in jail, but I wasn't interested in blackmail. A lot of things make Dean Rein a jerk, but having a fuckup for a son isn't one of them. I decided it was off-limits. See, I wasn't a bad person. Talia Pasteur was a bad person for using such a sad thing as blackmail.

From there, the emails mostly broke down the way I'd assumed they would. The emailer, who was calling herself Songbird (probably because Talia liked to sing, and her face was tiny and her nose was pointy), asked if Dean Rein wanted Astrid Krieger out of Bristol, and then she told him how to do it. What was interesting to me was that the "Songbird" emails didn't stop after I was kicked out. Songbird was still emailing Dean Rein. And it got weirder. Some emails were missing, but a month ago, Dean Rein wrote this: *I don't understand what you want or why you want this to happen, but I will allow Astrid Krieger to return to Bristol. However, after this I am done.*

I couldn't understand it. She wanted me out of Bristol, and then she wanted me back. None of my good deeds—nothing from my stupid list—had anything to do with it. It was Talia. I was walking into a trap that I didn't under-stand, and those were my least favorite kinds of traps. (My favorite traps were bear traps because they looked like shark smiles.)

The last email was from that morning. She said: *I need something else. You can't say no to me. When can we meet?*

It was starting to sound like Talia and Dean Rein were having secret sex rendezvous, but because the thought of that was so revolting that it was probably revolting to them too, it had to be impossible. I needed to figure out a new plan, and I had, like, a minute. I needed to find a person whom Dean Rein and Talia Pasteur would trust but who actually would be working for me. There was only one person I could think of who met all of those requirements. There was a picture on Dean Rein's desk of a man of about twenty-five on a fishing boat with wrap-around sunglasses and only one arm. Martin Rein Jr. I needed someone who could keep a secret and who could make Talia believe that she could tell him anything. I didn't know if this was true of Martin Jr., but I didn't need the real him. I just needed a man with one arm, which was easier to find than one might think (because everyone with two arms has one arm. It's called math, people).

I very quickly wrote an email to Songbird from Dean Rein's computer.

I heard movement and change jangling outside the door. Dean Rein was coming up the stairs. His shoes clomped on the floor outside his office just as I got a reply. It was quick and simple: *I'll be there*. It was all I needed.

When Dean Rein walked back into his office, the email had been deleted from his account and I was sitting on the other side of the room. He wouldn't have noticed anyway. His hands were covered in fake blood. Mason was in an ambulance. The paramedics soon figured out that they were in the middle of a prank, but before they could do anything about it, Mason ran away. Nobody ever figured out who he was or why he wanted anyone to believe he was trampled by a horse. Dean Rein never even heard about his escape.

My plan was just a notion at that point, but I had this image in my mind of how everything would end. I knew that I could pull it off. It wasn't satisfying enough just to clear my name. It wasn't satisfying enough to get Talia Pasteur kicked out of Bristol. I needed to do something bigger, for no other reason than that I was Astrid Krieger—and Astrid Krieger does things. But I also knew that I needed help. Getting help, as it turned out, was the easiest part of the whole thing. Nothing else was very easy at all.

## EXCERPTS FROM A BROCHURE FOR THE BRISTOL ACADEMY

**Founded in 1817 as a college devoted to shipbuilding, the Bristol Academy has developed into the nation's finest**

boarding school. Our most important mission is to nurture the leaders of tomorrow. Situated on the banks of Lake McCollum, Bristol challenges its students every day, while allowing them the opportunity to foster their independence by living away from home and building relationships that will last throughout their lives and careers.

>>>>>>>>>>>>>

## FREQUENTLY ASKED QUESTIONS ABOUT
## THE BRISTOL ACADEMY

*Is boarding school right for my child? We have always lived with our children.*

A lot of parents believe that sending their child away for school could mean that they love their child less and do not want them around. At Bristol, we believe differently. It is not selfish to send your child to a place where the best opportunities await. We understand that you lead a busy life, and so does your child. We believe that recognizing this early is a sign that you love your child even more.

*How is Bristol different from other schools? Isn't every student everywhere taking basically the same classes?*

It's different at Bristol. An average high school student

may take English, Social Studies, and Calculus, but Bristol additionally boasts classes such as Psychology, Philosophy, Chemical Engineering, and Classical Poetry. A student who excels at Bristol is already well versed in the curricula of the world's best universities. Our students are almost guaranteed a place at any college they want.

*My income makes it difficult for me to afford the tuition to Bristol. Do you offer scholarships for outstanding students?*
Unfortunately, no. Thank you for asking.

*What about athletics?*
Bristol boasts lengthy equestrian runs, a world-class squash court, and optional physical education classes taught by Olympic bronze medalist in bobsled racing Janusz Fijokwysky. Our students stay fit and healthy with meals prepared daily by a team of dietitians who discuss each individual student's nutritional needs.

*How many horses does Bristol have in the campus stables?*
At least twenty.

*Can you tell me about some of Bristol's best-known alumni?*
The Bristol Academy boasts a prestigious alumni roster that includes two US presidents, one vice president,

one Saudi Arabian prime minister, thirty-two Fortune 500 CEOs, eleven members of the US Congress, three Formula 1 racing world champions, one US poet laureate, two best-selling cookbook authors, and the co-songwriter of the seminal 1970s dance hit "Disco Zebra." Bristol students get to meet and network with many former students every year at our annual Boat Days and in the spring at the Festival of Blooms. Could the next great Bristol alumnus be your son or daughter?

# CHAPTER 26

# HOW MICROPHONES WORK

Boat Days is this giant student-alumni event. It is ridiculous for several reasons, but the most obvious are that it's only one day and it doesn't involve any boats. It's mostly a bunch of speeches and choral performances and finger food and old, fat assholes talking about a far-off time when they used to be young, thin assholes. Here's all you need to know: Boat Days is a big deal because it's when Bristol raises a lot of money, and it is the last day in the world that Dean Rein would want something bad to happen. So, naturally, when I was trying to figure out a plan to make something bad happen, there was really no better time to do it than Boat Days.

Two days before Boat Days, I had everyone come to my room. It was a very different group than I was used to, but I was impressed. Recruitment had been left in the hands of Lucy, and I hadn't thought she could handle it. But Lucy was a great recruiter. And I told her so.

She said, "All I said was that Astrid Krieger was going to do something big. Then I said, 'You can help or you can only hear about it.'"

"Do all of these people think I'm going to pay them?"

"They might." Lucy shrugged. "But it's not your responsibility to worry about what they think, is it?"

Lucy had brought together an unlikely group from Cadorette. People who, I had assumed, hated me. But there they were, sitting in various places on the floor of my room. Summer Wonder was in the corner. Next to her were the two girls who were always next to her. There was Beer Shirt (who actually wasn't wearing his beer shirt because Lucy told him he shouldn't) on the exact other side of the room. Mason brought Melty, who still looked terrified of me. Ben from the student council sat on the bed. From my world, Pierre was there because (as he put it) "Lovers support each other." I then asked him never, ever again to refer to us as *lovers* because my mouth filled with puke at the sound of the word. Since Boat Days was an event for Bristol alumni and I figured I needed a Bristol alumna, Lisbet was there.

Lisbet had never been a part of any of my plans. She said she was flattered I asked, but I could tell she was also confused. Lisbet didn't like to do bad things. I promised her that this plan wasn't bad. In fact, it was the enemy of bad. I was going to stop a bad person from doing bad things. I was like the police.

"Okay," she said. "But I won't steal anything or hit anyone or lie." I already knew this about Lisbet, and fortunately I didn't need her to do any of those things.

"I just need you to go to the alumni planning meeting." This was going to be easy for Lisbet. She was the president of her class at Bristol, and she was already a member of the planning committee. I wasn't asking her to do anything she wasn't doing already. The only change she had to make from how she was already leading her life was that she needed to volunteer to print the program of events.

"Oh," she said. "That's what Evangeline Roubaix is doing. I don't think I can step on her toes. You know she and I had that thing, Astrid." I didn't know who Evangeline Roubaix was or what that thing was. The old me would have probably told Lisbet her stupid problems didn't matter, and what I was saying was important, and she needed to understand that. But that wasn't the way I handled things anymore.

"Lisbet," I said, "I know this isn't the sort of thing you do. But I need you, and we're sisters. You're the only one who can help me with this specific problem of mine, and I wouldn't ask you if it wasn't important. You're my maid of honor, Lisbet, in life." This pretty much meant nothing, but I thought it was the sort of thing she would love to hear.

"Oh. I understand. Okay! What do you need me to do, exactly?"

"It's really simple. When you're doing the programs, there is one thing that's supposed to happen at two o'clock. I need you to change the program so it says it's happening at noon."

"That's it?"

"That's it," I said.

>>>>>>>>>>>>

I told Lucy that no one but she and I would know the entire plan. Otherwise, things like that get tricky because either you confuse people or they have some worthless idea about how to make the plan better. Instead, I told everyone privately what I needed them to do, and I told everyone the image I had for how the whole thing would end.

"It will be the middle of the day on Boat Days. There is a podium in the field by the lake. Dean Rein gives a speech. A freshman reads a poem. A senior says a few things about the future and all the wisdom he's collected in his life. The jazz band plays, and it sounds about as good and as bad as every jazz band has ever sounded. And then as a special treat, the students and alumni are going to hear a song performed by Bristol's choral group. The singers gather at the back of the stage, and the soloist walks to the microphone. She has this short, choppy blond hair and a lot of makeup. Her name is Talia Pasteur, and she is a bad person. She tried to ruin my life, and she deserves whatever is coming to her.

"She will open her mouth to sing, but she won't sing. Instead, she will step to the microphone and tell the crowd of fellow students and rich old alumni and everyone in this room right now that she is a liar, a thief, and a cheater. She will say that Astrid Krieger was set up and Talia will take all the blame. She will say that she coerced and manipulated Dean Rein to do whatever she wanted him to do. And the entire crowd will all agree that she deserves everything that is coming to her. And that's why you're all here. You're all going to make this happen."

Everyone looked a little stunned. Beer Shirt said, "Yeah. Okay. And how are we supposed to do that?"

"This plan is about microphones. Let me explain: When someone speaks into a microphone, we don't hear the things that are coming out of her mouth. The sound is coming out of speakers. The speakers could be all the way on the other side of, say, a field by a lake at a boarding school, but nobody doubts for a second that what's coming out of those speakers is the same thing that's coming out of the person's mouth. The plan isn't for someone else's voice to replace Talia's. That might work with someone else, but it wouldn't work with her. She has this way of speaking—this accent like she works in a speakeasy in the 1930s. Talia Pasteur's voice is like no other. She will actually have to say the things I need her to say or else it will never work. No one will ever believe her."

The ingenious part of the plan is that while I wasn't going to fake her voice, I was going to fake her face. When you get right down to it, the reason I thought she looked like a tree was that she wasn't noticeable. Her face was like every single face you've ever seen in your entire life. That was probably why she needed to work so hard to find a signature hairstyle and super-short clothes—because otherwise, no one would remember that Talia Pasteur had even existed. She looked like no one, and she looked like everyone. And for the sake of that particular plan, she looked like Summer Wonder—or at least enough like her to make it work.

When everyone left, Lucy stayed behind. I could tell that she was thinking hard because she sat cross-legged on my bed and both of her braids were lodged deeply in her jaw and she was looking up at the ceiling fan, following the blades with her eyes. When she finished thinking, she said the last thing I expected her to say. She said, "Astrid, this isn't going to work."

"Are you kidding me? You're telling me this now?" Lucy was the only person other than me who knew the whole plan start to finish. She had never said one negative thing about it the entire week. She just kept nodding. And then suddenly she said it wouldn't work. Her timing was just awful.

"Oh, you know, it's a good plan, Astrid. You're very smart. I can't believe you thought all of that up."

"But?"

"It's just one part. It's just one part that isn't going to work. But, you know, one thing falls apart and—"

"Boom," I said.

"Yeah. Boom."

"So, what is it?"

"So this Talia, she goes to the meeting with—"

"With Martin Rein Jr.," I said.

"Why is she going to tell him anything? I mean, Mason is great, but maybe not for this job." Mason had been excellent at pretending to be a Bristol student run over by a horse, so I had assumed he would be a natural for the part of Martin Jr. But to be fair, it was the least worked-out part of the entire plan and probably the most important.

"So, I'll get Beer Shirt to do it. Or Melty."

Talia shook her head. "She wants to be like you, right? This Talia wants to be you."

"I don't know about that—"

"She does," Lucy said. "And I would too. You're smart and pretty, and you always have a plan and an idea for everything. If she didn't want to be like you, she'd be an idiot. And if we need ten people to bring her down, she's not an idiot, right?"

I'm not a modest person, so I wasn't going to argue with Lucy about being smart and pretty and whether or not Talia wanted to be like me. I wasn't sure I believed it, but I didn't have the ability to step out of my body and look at myself, so I needed to take Lucy's word for it at that moment. "Fine," I said.

"You need Talia to trust someone and tell this person everything. If it was you, who would you trust?"

"I'll, um, I'll ask Pierre?"

Lucy rolled her eyes. "Please," she said. I still have no idea how she learned so much from me. Somehow I'd managed to teach Lucy what a waste of my time Pierre was while at the same time forgetting it myself. "If I needed to find someone you would tell everything to, who would that be?"

I knew exactly who that person would be. And I was really annoyed that Lucy was absolutely right. Goddamnit, I hated it when other people were right.

# CHAPTER 27

## CONSIDERING THAT I AM NOW A LITERARY CHARACTER, CAN I EXPECT A CAT TO BE DRESSED AS ME?

**I** always liked going to New York City. My grandfather would take me when I was so young, I probably shouldn't even remember it. We went to Midtown Manhattan, where the buildings were giant and men wearing red jackets held open the door. There were rooms filled with steaks and leather, and I sat on my grandfather's lap while he drank golden glasses of whiskey. He would tell me then, "This glass of whiskey is just about the only thing worthwhile in the entire world."

Noah didn't live in that part of New York. He lived in Brooklyn. It was a part of Brooklyn that was accessible only by taking multiple trains and walking eight blocks and climbing five flights of stairs. The building smelled like Chinese food, and your feet stuck to the floor when you walked.

When I first searched for Noah Einstein, the only results Google produced were about bagels. That's why I didn't find out that Noah was only pretending to be a high school student until it was too late. He was hard to locate. But then I remembered his website—cats dressed like literary characters—and as it turned out, it actually existed. Not everything he'd ever told me was a lie, apparently. I found the domain registry, and the home address brought me to his apartment. I wasn't very happy about it, but I went there anyway.

A large guy with a greasy face opened the door. He had a cat under one arm and a powdered wig and a Victorian collar in his fist. It was clear that weird stuff went on in that apartment. "My name's Jake," the greasy guy said.

"Oh. I'm—"

"You're Astrid Krieger."

"So I am."

"Yeah, I know who you are. I figured you'd come here eventually. He said you wouldn't. I don't even know you, but I still knew you would. He called. You saw he tried to call, right? Don't be too hard on him, okay? He's not that bad." He called out to the back of the apartment, which was about the size of a small thumbnail. "Noah!"

And then Noah was right there.

I decided to get right to it. "Listen. I'm not here to settle anything. I'm still mad at you. I don't think I'll ever stop being mad at you. If you can't deal with that, fine.

But I need your help with something. I wouldn't be here if I didn't absolutely need your help. So—"

And just like that, Noah was out the door. "Of course," he said. "I'll do whatever you need, Astrid."

>>>>>>>>>>>>

We walked to the subway station, took the two trains to Grand Central Station, and from there the Metro-North to West Ashton and a taxi to Southboro to the front gate of Bristol. All in all, we went about eighty miles and it took us, I don't know, seventy-three hours. That's an exaggeration, but it felt like forever.

We didn't talk for the first nine days of our journey to Bristol (again, an exaggeration, but those trains sure are slow). Eventually, though, Noah started talking.

"I need to explain some things," he said.

"I'm not interested in listening."

"Well, just let me talk. You don't have to listen."

"My ears aren't eyes."

"Huh?" he said.

"I can't close them." I turned away from him, but I listened.

"So after I graduated from high school, I began to work at Krieger Industries. It was this program that my high school guidance counselor found where you intern for a scholarship. I didn't know too much about the place, other than the really negative things, but my guidance counselor told me that there was no such thing as a good company, and it was a way for me to pay for college. It was the first of a few things I have done that didn't feel right, but I did them anyway. I did what I needed to do for me. You of all people have to understand that.

"I worked through the summer. I saw you a few times. You came in some afternoons. You used the copy machine and would say things like, 'The receptionist's sweater makes it look like she's being strangled by a parrot.'"

"Yeah," I said. "That sounds like me."

"Those were some of the few interesting moments of the entire summer. Most days, I would sort mail. And get coffee. And then get mail. And sort coffee.

"But one day, my supervisor said that the boss wanted to see me. I had no idea what boss he was referring to. Everybody who worked there was basically my boss. I was the least important person in the whole company. I was surprised when I was brought into your father's office. He wasn't paying attention to me. He was playing with a model airplane."

"That's pretty much all he does. Sometimes he wanders around the office telling his employees how to make a perfect cup of coffee. He's always like, 'You don't have to smell a coffee bean to know how it's going to taste.'"

"I thought you weren't listening."

"Well, I don't know what he means when he says that, so it's not like I'm helping you," I said and turned my head back away from him.

"Your grandfather was in a wheelchair near a bookshelf in your father's office, and he asked if I could push him around so we could talk. He asked me what I thought of this place, the company. I don't know what came over me, but I told him the truth. He had this way about him; I knew he would see right through me if I lied. I said, 'I think what you do here is basically evil. I'm bored to death and I work here because I was out of options.' So he said, 'Good, you're perfect. I got a special job for you.'

"It's like one of those be-careful-what-you-wish-for things, because nothing was worse for me than high school. I was only a year out, and now I was going back. I thought it was worth it, but I still didn't feel good about it. When I was in school, kids threw garbage at my head. My nickname was 'Gay Noah,' even though there was another kid named Noah and he actually was gay. I hoped that going to this school wouldn't be as bad. It turned out to be worse, but for a different reason. Your grandfather's people forged a transcript saying I was younger than I was, and I started school. I knew I was doing the wrong thing the moment I saw you in that class. I knew that I didn't want to lie to you. But I did it. I did it every day. I could've stopped. I could've quit. But I didn't.

"He didn't tell me why I was watching you. At least at first. He just said I needed to be your friend, listen to you, keep an eye on you. And then when you went to the bar before your sister's wedding, he told me. He said he was dying. He had a bad heart, and he needed surgery. Instead of getting the surgery, he'd decided that he was done. He was ready. His only regret was you. He'd spent the duration of your life teaching you how to be like him, and then he looked at himself and he was sorry. He had been wrong. You were better than he was. He needed to fix it before he was gone. He sent you to public school, made a lot of rules, and hired me. He thought all that together could stop the damage he'd caused.

"He said, 'If I'm gone soon, I need you to tell her something.'"

I perked up and turned my head toward Noah, who was looking right at me.

"I asked if I should write it down," he said, "but he said that I should remember it. I hope I did.

"So your grandfather told me, 'I was always alone. And that was fine with me, but then suddenly it wasn't fine anymore. I was wrong about that. That's one. I took things my whole life, but in the end, I just have things. Should've given more. Should have done more. Shouldn't have been such an ornery asshole. That's two. I love that kid, and I'm going to miss her when I'm gone. I wish I didn't push people away. I hope she doesn't do the same. I never thought I would ever care about anyone more than I care about me. But that's no longer true, is it? Surprises me every single day. That's three.'

"And then he said, 'Astrid, she's going to be better. She'll do whatever she wants. And whatever that is, watch out, 'cause it's going to be great. She should let herself care about things. She's gonna matter. He then said to tell you, 'I love you, Monkey. Always.'"

I smiled and rested my head on Noah's shoulder.

"He said that my business with him was done. He took out his checkbook and said that he could make sure I never had to worry about money again."

"You made a wise business decision," I said.

"Did I?" he asked.

"Someone should cash in on my grandfather's offer. I never wanted to see you again anyway. I'm glad you got paid."

"I didn't take the money," he said.

"That's stupid. You're a terrible businessman, Noah. A

real idiot." And then I said, "Thank you."

"I screwed everything up," he said. "I know I did. I screwed everything up with you. With everything."

I nodded. He was right. He did screw a lot up.

"I hope whatever it is you need my help to do, it's not too hard because I'll probably screw that up too."

"Too bad," I said. "It's probably the most important part of the entire plan."

# CHAPTER 28

# BOAT DAYS

Lisbet had a hard time acting the part of Lisbet in the alumni meeting at the beginning of the day. I reminded her that she called herself an actress, and playing herself should have been much easier than playing someone else. She told me that I didn't understand the craft of acting, and she would be able to get a handle on it if I allowed her to do it with a British accent. I decided that while this was very weird, sure, whatever, who cares. Lisbet would simply have to explain to Evangeline Roubaix and whoever else was in the meeting why she was suddenly from a different country. She told me that challenges like that were what made theater interesting.

I wrote out a small index card of what Lisbet needed to say, and even then I wasn't sure she could handle it. Lisbet's job was the easiest thing anyone had to do for the entire day. Thankfully, that part ended up working, so maybe I hadn't given her enough credit. In a soft British accent, she raised her hand and said, "The ceremony can't be at two. It needs to be at eleven thirty. Because of the sun. It shan't be too cold." Not brilliant stuff, by any means, but she did what she had to do.

>>>>>>>>>>>>>

More than anything, I needed Pierre out of my way. It was nice of him to want to help, but I needed to keep him busy so he didn't spend the whole day rubbing my shoulders. That was a thing he liked to do. I didn't know why. It didn't make my shoulders feel any better, as his massage technique felt like Velcro on a melon.

So I told him it was essential to my plan that he spend the morning putting together a picnic. And he did. He made a basket full of sandwiches. And then he ate them.

Noah and I couldn't quite decide how he should look, considering neither of us knew Martin Rein Jr. In pictures, Martin Jr. wore a scarf and sunglasses even when he was inside. He wore madras boat pants and wing tip shoes.

Noah assured me that if he was wearing any of those things, nobody would believe for a second that he was anything but a person in a costume. Noah said that he couldn't even wear a baseball hat without looking like one of those little kids who had to wear a helmet because the back of their head was flat. After a little bit of debate, it was decided that Noah would go to the meeting looking pretty much exactly like himself, but with his arm inside his jacket sleeve.

"Do you know what to say?" I asked.

"I hope so," Noah said.

I'm not sure why Ben, Cadorette Township's student council president, wanted to help me at all. We weren't friends, and he didn't owe me a favor. He said he had always wanted to visit Bristol because the poet Yoseph Blahblahblah teaches there. That's not the name he said, but I lost interest after he said "poet."

I told him that he didn't have to help. He could just leave and listen to poetry, but he said, "No, you need someone who understands sound equipment." He said he understood that stuff intimately "because of all the gigs I play with my band, Wandering Baskets of Rainbow Bear Destruction Hula Hoop Sunglasses." Okay, I made that name up, but it was something like that. He had more expertise in microphones and soundboards than I did. I only really understood them as ideas.

He attached a lavalier microphone to the inside of

Noah's jacket and said, "It's a go." That was microphone talk.

Ben hooked a receiver to the soundboard in front of the stage. Moments after noon, he was to turn the receiver on. A simple switch. The sound coming into the lavalier microphone on the other side of the campus would then take over.

Joe Flemming was running the soundboard for the day, and while I'd known him for as long as I'd been at Bristol, I'd never known that much about him. I knew he was good at technology, and I knew that he was loyal to me no more and no less than he was to whoever else paid him.

Beer Shirt (who, again, wasn't wearing an actual beer shirt) sat down next to Joe Flemming. I told him a bunch of things that he could say. I told him to be threatening, but not too threatening. It never got that far. He said, "I'm sitting here now."

And Joe Flemming said, "Fine with me." And he left.

Summer Wonder wore a short, choppy wig. She was wearing short shorts and a T-shirt where one side was on her shoulder and the other side was off the shoulder.

I had a picture of Talia, which I showed to Summer's friend with the red hair. I said, "Make her look as horrible as this."

The redhead said, "Really? I like this. I think this girl is pretty."

So I said, "Fine, then. Make her look exactly this pretty."

I asked Lucy if she'd ever done any breaking and entering before. She laughed until she realized I was serious. She hadn't, and I told her that I wasn't going to make her join me. I didn't want her to get in trouble for anything that had nothing to do with her. I didn't know how an arrest record would look on a college application. (I do know now, but only with my own arrest record and my own college applications. It doesn't look great, but you can sometimes talk your way around it if you are as persuasive and charming as I am.)

Lucy said that she didn't mind. She found all of this exciting.

"Are we going to steal something?" Lucy wanted to know.

"Breaking and entering is a waste of time if you're not going to steal something," I said.

Mason stood in the bushes near the chapel with Melty. I called it running surveillance. Mason was standing in a hedge with his younger brother's walkie-talkie. It was covered in crayon marks. We certainly weren't the CIA, but Mason and Melty's task was still important.

Across the campus, I wore a lumpy earpiece. I needed to know what was happening on the other side of campus even though it mostly sounded like static and an AM Christian talk radio station that I picked up only half the time. I wondered for a moment how I'd fallen so far.

In my earpiece, I could hear Dean Rein welcome the students and alumni. His speech was about the future, the past, mountain climbing, eagles, brains, and money. If no one stopped him, he might have still been giving that speech. After seven minutes, his microphone started making this horrible noise. It was the sound of cats dying and/or making love. Ben made it sound like an accident, a weird technical glitch. But it shut Dean Rein up. He turned the assembly over to the freshman and his poem.

I had the metal part of the cap of a Uni-Ball Roller in one hand (an excellent lock-picking tool, and they are not paying me for the endorsement), and I was wiggling a paper clip with the other. Lock picking is an art. But, as with any sort of art, sometimes it happened, sometimes it didn't. This lock was not happening. I had been wiggling pieces of metal around for three minutes, and I was running out of time. If I had had my campus master key, I wouldn't have had this problem. But the campus master key was precisely what we were stealing from Talia's room. The master key I had bribed a janitor for my first year at Bristol had gone missing the previous year. For someone to get their hands on those old tests that had been sent to Dean Rein, they must have that key. I never kept the tests. I shredded them, along with all copies. To compile that evidence, someone would have needed access to faculty lounges, computer labs, copy rooms, and file cabinets. I had decided that Talia stole my key. That was how she orchestrated my expulsion. I needed that key back. If by tomorrow I would once again be at the top of Bristol, I needed the means to go wherever I wanted.

"This used to be your room, right?" Lucy said.

"I'm trying to concentrate, Lucy."

"I know. I'm sorry. I'm just saying that, well, maybe they didn't change the lock."

Lucy was smarter than I gave her credit for. She was right. You don't always need the key that unlocks every door. Not if you have the key that unlocks the door you need unlocked. It was good advice for a lot of situations that weren't even about keys and doors.

I took my key chain out of my bag. The dorm key was still there.

"For a rich girl," Lucy said, "you have a lot of keys."

>>>>>>>>>>>>

At the exact same time that Talia Pasteur was supposed
to be across campus having a secret meeting with Dean
Rein's son, Dean Rein called Talia Pasteur to the stage.
The program said that she was going to sing a song. It was
supposed to be something from *The Little Mermaid*. Talia
herself thought she was supposed to take the stage at two.
No one had told her that the ceremony had been switched.
Lisbet had made sure of that, just as I had instructed her.

Nobody watching the stage had any idea that the girl
walking to the microphone wasn't Talia Pasteur. Those
who knew her recognized her short blond hair and her
makeup. They were about to hear her voice, and anyone
who knew her knew her voice. Way after the events of
that day, people still had no idea that the girl in front of
the microphone wasn't Talia Pasteur. Even though everyone now knows how poorly my plan went, the fact that
an essential detail ended up working was actually kind of
impressive.

Noah stood behind a tree until it was time for his role.
He took a deep breath, and then he walked out of the
shadows to meet Talia Pasteur.

At the very same time, I slid my key into my old dorm

room's door and opened it. Lucy and I walked inside.

"So where is this master key?" Lucy asked.

"I can't be sure, but I know where *I* kept it." There was a small compartment in the headboard of the bed. No one would ever find it unless they lived in that room. I never got to check, though. I never got past the bed. Talia Pasteur wasn't meeting anyone outside the chapel. Talia Pasteur wasn't singing a song from *The Little Mermaid*. Talia Pasteur was sitting in her room, staring at me.

I heard a rumbling of static, a Bible verse, and the tail end of whatever Mason was saying in my ear. Specifically, I heard "SHHHHHHHHH—ye also are become dead to the law by the body of Christ— . . . not what was supposed to happen, Astrid."

"What are you doing here?" I said to Talia. I knew I wasn't making a lot of sense to her. This was her room.

"This is my room," she said. I could tell myself whatever I wanted, but nothing changed the fact that the corner room on the top floor of Ladies' Dorm 3 was no longer my room. Talia Pasteur lived there. Her stupid clothes and stupid posters and stuffed dolphins (seriously) were all over the place. It smelled like strawberry candles. I was working so hard to take back whatever it was that I felt she had of mine, but standing there right then, I thought it didn't seem all that great. None of those things would be in my room, which was as much proof as anything that this wasn't my room anymore.

"It's twelve o'clock," Lucy said. "Isn't she supposed to be at the chapel?"

"Who's this person?" Talia asked.

"She's with me."

"Tell her to leave. The grown-ups are talking," Talia said.

"She's staying. I said she was with me."

"Well, tell her to get her hair out of her mouth. It's absolutely disgusting."

"That's what she does," I said. "We all have our things, don't we?" Lucy smiled.

"So what do you want to talk about?" Talia demanded. "Tell me already, and let's get on with our stupid lives."

I wanted to say a lot of things to Talia. Some were factual. Some mean. But it wasn't going to get me anywhere. I knew what the right thing to say was. It was something I didn't want to do, but I did it anyway. I said, "Talia, I'm sorry."

"What are you sorry for?"

"I know you don't like me. I get that. There a lot of people in the world who have a lot more reasons to hate me than you. But you're right. I should've been nicer to you. I should've listened to you. I should've considered you. I should've done better. And I'm sorry. But the thing I still don't understand is, why did you get me kicked out?"

Talia didn't even change her expression. She moved her shoulders a little bit and said, "Thank you for apologizing. But you must know by now I didn't get you kicked out of Bristol. It wasn't me."

It took until that moment for me to really think about what little I knew about the person who wrote those emails and sent those tests to Dean Rein. I had just assumed it was Talia Pasteur because of the way her life had seemed to change so much when I left. Like she had been waiting forever to be someone else. Like she'd been planning on it. But seeing her right then, I realized that her life was nothing special. Nothing to plan for. I looked outside the window, and I saw people laughing and talking and having their days. Talia was in her room all alone.

"If it wasn't you, who was it?" I asked.

"You don't know?" she asked, incredulous. "You really don't know?"

# CHAPTER 29

# BAM

The plan failed. It went nothing like I thought it would. When Summer Wonder, dressed as Talia Pasteur, stood in front of the microphone and opened her mouth, the voice of Talia Pasteur did not come out. Instead, the assembled crowd heard someone else. I still think my idea about tricking people with microphones was a good idea. I still think it would have worked in a different situation. But in this instance, nope. Nobody thought the voices coming out of the speakers belonged to the girl onstage. Everyone who didn't know what was actually happening was more confused than anything else. They were expecting to hear a song from *The Little Mermaid*. Everyone working for me expected to hear Talia's confession. Instead, the confession they heard was Pierre's.

>>>>>>>>>>>>

Just a little after noon, Noah—a man temporarily with one arm—stepped out from behind the tree. When he saw Pierre waiting for him, he didn't immediately figure out what was happening. That was okay because it took me a moment to figure it out too. Noah assumed that this was just part of the plan, that I had asked Pierre to come along. But it was Pierre he was supposed to be waiting for the whole time.

Pierre was the one who had sent those emails to Dean Rein. Pierre got me kicked out of Bristol. Pierre wanted to see me fail.

Why did he do it? Well, everyone knows that now. As soon as Noah realized that Pierre's presence wasn't part of the plan, it was the first thing he asked, and it was the first thing the crowd heard over the loudspeaker. "It was you. Why would you do that?" Noah said. "Why would you do that to her?"

And then they heard Pierre say: "The first time I saw her, she was across the dining room. She was sitting in the corner by herself. I sat down next to her. I said, 'I see you are here all alone. Can I offer you some of my company?'

"She said something similar to 'Please leave, or else I will throw my food at you.' I could not help it. Love is something you cannot control. Perhaps if I had a choice, I would love somebody else. But I do not believe I have had a choice. Instead, I have spent years hoping there would be a way for me. That was why I did this. Maybe you cannot understand something like that, but it was the only way. She had to leave this school. Because she will never love me the way that she is. You know how she is. You know her too. She was always too good for everything in the world. She was too good for me. She said things like that. But if she wasn't too good for everything, then *maybe*, I thought. Maybe if I—what do you call it?—take her down all the notches. If I punished her, maybe she would be able to see me. It was the only way to do it. You understand. You must understand."

There was silence for a minute, and everyone wondered what was going on when they couldn't hear anything. Then Noah finally spoke. "I don't believe a word you're saying. I mean, I believe the events you describe, but your story, it's meaningless. It's stupid, and you're wrong. You say you love her. You don't love her. You love how being in love feels, maybe. You love telling people that you love her. But you couldn't love her. If you loved her, you would want to see her be great. You would want to be there when she does great things. You would be there for her when she doesn't. You don't deserve her. You don't understand her. You don't love her at all. And she knows that. She's much smarter than you. She's much smarter than me. I hope you're happy now. You did all of this, and it didn't even work."

I could hear Pierre smiling. I could hear it because he makes a noise like he's having trouble breathing out of the sides of his mouth when he smiles. He said, "But, don't you know? It did work. It worked for me. See, it is okay that she cannot love me. I never needed that. It is not what I asked for, and it did work. She didn't tell you? She is my girlfriend now. I hold her hand. I kiss her at the end of the night. She is my girlfriend. It did work. It worked better than I had hoped."

>>>>>>>>>>>>

I was standing at the back of the crowd at that point. I was basically invisible. Everything was happening in front of me. I caught Dean Rein's eye. He shook his head. I shrugged.

Dean Rein said, "How did I know that somehow today was going to be about you?"

"It could have been worse," I said.

"I'm not sure. I don't know what's going to happen next."

"I think I do," I said and looked toward the chapel.

"Are you okay, Astrid? Your face is red."

"Yeah, it's, like, burning. It's been happening." I started to run to the other side of campus. There, two boys were talking about me. One of them I actually cared about. The other one was my boyfriend. My face felt hotter and hotter. It was a familiar feeling, one I didn't like at all. I was out of place. Everything was blurry. The last thing I could make out was Noah, just before I fell into his head. Again.

BAM!

>>>>>>>>>>>>

When I woke up, a few people had gathered, and both Noah and I were on the ground.

"They were like this," Pierre said. "I did not touch him. I did not put a hand on him."

I pulled myself up into a kneeling position and scooted over toward Noah. He was dirty, and there was a scrape on his head, but he was breathing and blinking. One of his arms was clutching a tree root. The other was still hidden in his jacket.

"I did nothing," Pierre said. "Nothing."

"Go away, Pierre," I said.

"Astrid."

"Don't look at me. Ever. Don't talk to me. Ever. Go

away!" It wasn't just a demand. It was a scream. Everyone could hear me.

Pierre wasn't sad or anything. For all the bullshit he liked to say about what a caring, loving person he was, he didn't look heartbroken. He looked angry. His jaw was tight. His face was red. He said, "I wish you didn't say that." I wasn't sure what he was going to do next.

I heard Noah moving in the dirt. He shifted and slowly pulled himself up. Pierre squeezed his hand into a fist. Noah turned to me, standing then. "Remember when I told you why I don't fight back?"

"Yeah," I said.

And then Noah ran at Pierre and yelled something like, "AHHHHHH!"

There was this blur of motion. I never expected it to turn into a fistfight because Pierre was wearing a shirt that had actual shoulder pads and Noah was . . . you know, Noah. Though at that moment, Noah didn't look the same. He was scraped and filthy, and his arms were just pounding into Pierre. Sometimes Noah was a feather of a person, but at that moment he seemed stronger. It was nice to see someone stand up for me. I hoped he didn't hurt himself, but I couldn't remember another time when I hadn't had to stand up for myself.

Pierre was on the ground, and little bits of blood were

leaking from his nose. Finally I grabbed Noah's shoulder. "Enough," I told him, and he pulled away.

"I did care about you, Astrid," Pierre said.

"You don't care about anything," I said.

"If that is true, at least it means we are the same. You only care about yourself. It is why we are so right for each other." Pierre let that sit in the air for a moment.

I turned back to look at Noah. He held his palm up as if to push Pierre, even though they were ten feet apart. "You should go," he said.

Pierre had no response. He just stood up and ran away.

>>>>>>>>>>>>

"Are you okay?" I asked Noah.

Noah mumbled something I couldn't understand, and then he said, "Was that true?"

"Was what true?"

"Is he your boyfriend?" Noah said.

"It's true, Noah," I said. Yes, I was letting Pierre call me his girlfriend. Or, if I was being honest with myself, I was Pierre's girlfriend. Maybe he tricked me into it. But I fell for the trick, so that was the reality, and there was no reason to lie about it. "At least, it was true until ten seconds ago. Not anymore. Can I explain?"

"You don't need to explain."

"I need to explain it to you."

"Did you care about him?" he said.

I shook my head.

"I don't think you two are the same," he said. "I don't think you only care about yourself. Maybe I'm just naive, but I think you care a lot. Your grandfather thought so too."

Noah came into my life as a confederate, a liar, and a spy. But there we were, and I didn't really care about any of that stuff anymore. With Noah, I don't know—standing there in that moment, I could pretty much tell who he was and what really mattered. He wasn't lying to me anymore. And I knew that whatever I decided I wanted to do, he would probably stand with me on my way there. I could tell that right then. I was good at figuring out what people were good at.

This is the part of the story where I should have told Noah something like, *I love you. I think I've always loved you. I didn't realize it until this moment, but we are made for each other.*

But that part didn't happen. Why? Because I wasn't a stupid moron. At that point, I had known Noah for almost no time at all. And for most of that, I didn't actually know too much about him. I had only known that he was older than I thought he was and that he was sent to Cadorette for me. I was way too sensible to let myself feel something like love for someone I knew so little about. Maybe some people can't buy a sandwich without falling in love with three people, but those people are weird. What I felt right then was a big deal for me. I did feel something very strong and very different, and it was the sort of feeling I frankly hadn't thought I was capable of having.

"Noah," I said, "I think I like you very much."

He smiled. It was enough for him and enough for me.

He put his hand on my shoulder. His hand was cold, and I was feeling strangely warm and thirsty. I had kissed boys before, but it was always because I wanted something or I couldn't think of something better to do. That moment was different. All I actually wanted was the kiss. Our faces moved closer, and our lips touched, and boom. We were two people attached by our lips. (Which, if you really thought about it, wasn't that romantic and was actually a little gross.) A kiss is treating a person exactly as intimately as you would treat licorice or a stamp. But how it looks is different from how it feels. I liked how it felt. It felt soft, and it made my mouth tingle, and my breathing changed entirely. It felt like receiving a pretty fantastic gift (a katana sword? Or a baby elephant?). There was something about the whole thing that felt like it was the right thing to do at that exact moment. It had been a long time since I'd done something that felt exactly right at the exact right moment.

I can't say how long the kiss took. It honestly could have been just a few seconds. Kisses are the sorts of things that shouldn't go too long or you kill the moment and your jaw starts to hurt, and your lips get chapped, and you look at the person you kissed and think, *Why the hell did you do this to me?* But this one couldn't have gone that long because not a lot of time could have passed before we started smelling the smoke.

It made both of us cough. We turned away from the kiss at the exact same time and hacked and gasped and beat each other's backs. You know, romantic. Swoon.

At first it was an invisible smell. Then we were surrounded very quickly by this grey cloud. I could feel the whole place getting much, much hotter. Right in front of us was the chapel. And the chapel was on fire.

# CHAPTER 30

# FIRECRACKER PART II

**N**obody should ever say that they love fire because that's just a crazy thing to say. People will look at you like you said, *My hobby is stabbing*, or, *Let me tell you another interesting thing about my pet ferret*. But even though nobody wants to admit they love a fire, everybody—and I mean everybody—will come out to watch something burn.

The chapel was ON FIRE IN ALL CAPITAL LETTERS. Maybe seven fire trucks showed up. They were able to do nothing but make sure the rest of the school didn't also burn down. The chapel was done for. It was built in the 1880s. It was made of brick and, apparently, some really dry wood. Everyone at Boat Days stood as close as the firefighters allowed and watched the building become this giant, red-and-orange, smoky monster.

When people remember that day, they won't think about Pierre, Talia, my grandfather, Lucy, Noah, or even me. That's because the day ended in a fire. And a fire beats everything. You know why they don't call the game Rock Paper Scissors *Fire*? Because not only would fire win in every situation, but it would be no fun playing a game where your friend could set your hand on fire.

Fire is fierce. Fire is angry. Fire does whatever it fucking wants. I am a big fan of fire.

When the firefighters rolled up their hoses, it was about one in the morning. It had been a long day, and almost nobody had left. It was something pretty great to watch. I only left because I felt a tap on my shoulder. It was Dean Rein. He said, "You. Come with me. Now."

>>>>>>>>>>>>>

Talia Pasteur and Pierre were already sitting in chairs outside Dean Rein's office. I could feel them both eyeing me as I crossed the room. I did what I always did in situations like that one—I pretended that I knew exactly what I was doing there. But to be honest, I had no idea.

I'd been called to Dean Rein's office probably a thousand times before. It wasn't always Dean Rein who called me in, but it was always someone like Dean Rein. It was a headmaster, a teacher, a lawyer, the head of security at the Berlin Zoo (in Germany they call lions *Löwen*. It's a scarier word). It was all pretty much the same. I knew what to do. But Dean Rein wasn't planning on fighting that night.

He looked like he'd had a long day, and it was turning into a long night. Whatever happened before I got there had made him impatient. He was holding a pen and tapping it really fast on his desk. With his other hand, he slapped an alternate beat. I wasn't sure what kind of music Dean Rein listened to, but I could tell that I wouldn't have liked it. "Let's talk turkey," he said. "I won't insult you by playing games."

"I love playing games," I said. "I'm surprised you don't know that about me."

He shook his head. "I have headaches, Astrid. All sorts of headaches. This fire—this is not good for me. And if it's not good for me, it's not good for anyone."

"It was good for the firemen. They probably made a lot of money on that one."

He sighed. He really *wasn't* interested in playing games. "That's not how firemen get paid."

"They should. It would make them work harder. If there had been something to gain, maybe they would have put that thing out a little sooner. But why do they care? A paycheck's a paycheck."

Dean Rein leaned in close like he was going to tell

me a super-private secret. "Listen, I know there are things you want. I know you could be happier at Bristol. What would you say to getting your own room back? How about a class schedule a little more to your liking? I'm sure there are some other things too. Everything is negotiable."

"Okay. It's a deal. Once again, a pleasure doing business with you."

"Not so fast. This is where I tell you what I want in return."

"Oh." I rolled my eyes. "Great."

"You'll like this too. I happen to know there are some people you'd prefer to not have around here anymore. If I was to guess, I would say your life might be improved if perhaps the young lady and the young man sitting outside that door no longer attended this school."

"Yeah, those guys. They're the worst. The absolute worst."

"I'm glad to hear you're thinking that way. So, let's say you scratch my back and I'll scratch yours."

"Oh, I hope you don't mean that literally. I imagine yours is all sweaty and hairy."

"Enough."

"It's probably got red blotches."

"My back is fine."

"It's not a fair trade-off. My back is great. It's soft and slender—"

"You know what I mean. You know it's a figure of speech. Let's just get this conversation over with, okay?"

"So what do you want, exactly?"

"Just tell me what you know. I know you know who started the fire. Just tell me."

"I'm not a rat."

"Who's calling you a rat? Think of yourself as a businesswoman. This is just a negotiation." He opened a drawer and took out a key. It wasn't just any key, of course. I knew it very well. It was the master key to the school. *My* master key. And it was beautiful. "It was in the chapel door. The firemen found it. I'm positive you know which of those two used it to get in there and set the fire."

I didn't say anything. Not yet.

"Come on," he said. "Just tell me. Who was it?"

The truth was, I had no idea who set the chapel on fire. Pierre had been angry after he walked away from Noah and me. Talia Pasteur was in love with Pierre, and she just heard him tell the whole school once and for all that he loved me. I'm not sure what the purpose of the fire was, but then, I had never been one for destruction for destruction's sake. I'd always needed things to have a purpose, and the chapel fire, well, it just had no style. It was a tacky move, and I hated tacky.

But the more important question was, what did I actually want from Dean Rein? What did I want at all anymore? What was I fighting for? I tried to evaluate my life for the next six months of my senior year at Bristol and I didn't like how it looked. It wasn't me. Not anymore. That world was for the Pierres and the Talia Pasteurs. Those two deserved each other. They deserved to be miserable, and they were destined for a special misery that I didn't need to control. They had the rest of their ordinary lives right ahead of them.

And whatever my life was, I didn't want any more of it to be at Bristol. I knew that there was only one way to answer Dean Rein. And when I made the decision in my mind, it felt right. I felt a wave of positive emotions coursing around in my head. I started grinning uncontrollably. I was happy.

"It was me," I said.

"What?"

"That's my key. I used it to open the chapel. I walked inside, and I lit a match, and I burned it down. That's what I did. If there is a fire to start, I will always start it. That's what I do."

Dean Rein didn't look mad or anything. He was truly

confused. He really thought that I was no longer a person who would do anything like that. I guess that was one point in his favor—which made our score nine hundred ninety-nine to one.

"You know I have to expel you, Astrid. Again."

"I figured." I was almost laughing at that point, which confused him even more. I couldn't control being happy. It was all out there, and it was hilarious.

"But this isn't just about Bristol," he said. "You may very well be in serious trouble. I have to call the police, of course. You may have to go to jail for this."

"I've been to jail," I said. "It's surprisingly not that bad at all."

Dean Rein leaned back in his chair and looked out the window. It was dark outside, so he was looking at absolutely nothing. "Why?" he asked. "Why did you do it?"

I leaned in close to him as if to impart a secret. "The world turned and flung me," I said. And then I winked.

Dean Rein's mouth made what could only be described as a smile in return. "I've heard a lot of excuses. That's an interesting one." I may have made his life miserable, but I was certainly entertaining. "Do you have anything else to say, Astrid?"

"I like how your toupee looks," I said. "It's very believable."

"I don't wear a toupee," he said.

"I know. It's *very* believable."

>>>>>>>>>>>>>

I walked out of his office, and a crowd of people were waiting. Some I knew. Some were the kids who had come that day to help me. They were my friends.

I found Noah and told him, "I think I understand why people do good things."

"Okay. I'll bite. Why?"

"I think it's something about people," I said. "You know, the more that people surround you, the more good you want to do."

"Are you talking about yourself?" he said.

"Do you think I'm a good person?"

"You're a great person," he said.

I happened to always think I was a great person. I never doubted that part for a second. A good person? Well, I'd never been sure. But that was only because it was hard to do good things, and it wasn't always fun. In fact, it sometimes sucked—but when you did it enough, it was in your DNA. It became who you were.

When you get to your last year of high school, everyone you've ever met in your entire life asks you, *What are you going to do next?* Noah and I had an understanding that he would never ask that question again. We talked about things. We talked about jobs and cities and directions, but I had no plan. I had no idea what was going to happen next. I was actually okay with that.

We both knew that the moment we were in was temporary. (At least I hoped so. Wouldn't it be horrible to spend eternity next to a smoldering building at your school?) The year would eventually end, and we would both go on to other places. Maybe for me, it would be an airport or a train station or a college dorm. Maybe I would step out of Noah's terrible car, and he would let go of my hand.

"Take care of yourself, Astrid," he would say.

And then I would say, "I always do."